Kalidas was one among the navratnas in the court of emperor Vikramaditya. He is considered an outstanding poet of the Sanskrit literature. All of his poetic compositions have received accolades from poetic scholars. Nevertheless the wonder that his literary talent has exhibited in the thespian composition 'Abhigyan Shakuntalam' is unmatched.

This work has been translated into several languages of the world and the connoisseurs of those languages derive great delight from it.

This English translation of Kalidas' eternal and matchless composition is presented for the fond readers of English language.

Kalidas'

Abhigyan Shakuntalam

Ashok Kaushik

Publisher : **Diamond Pocket Books (P) Ltd.**
X-30, Okhla Industrial Area, Phase-II
New Delhi - 110020
Phone : 011-40712200
E-mail : sales@dpb.in
Website : www.diamondbook.in
Translated by: : Sanjay Shrivastava

ABHIGYAN SHAKUNTALAM
Ashok Kaushik

Quote Unquote

The great German poet, Gete, had stated once, "If you want to find the flowers of youth and fruits of the middle age at one place, or if you want to collect such material as would influence the soul, satiate it and also give eternal peace to it—which means if you want to see heaven and earth at one place—then, only one name automatically comes to my mind. That name is *Abhigyan Shakuntalam*. It is, no doubt, one of the immortal pieces of literary work of the great poet — Kalidas!"

Preface

Kalidas' position in the Sanskrit literature is unequalled. Kalidas was one among the *navratnas* (nine jewels) of emperor Vikramaditya. The cabinet of ministers of the emperors during olden times used to be called their *ratnamandal* (galaxy of jewels). Ministers were akin to jewels in those times. It is difficult to say who was more bright, brilliant and influential than who among the *navratnas* of Vikramaditya. As Kalidas holds a unique position in the Sanskrit literature, his position was also unique in the ministerial cabinet of Vikramaditya.

A lot has been said about the narrative compositions of Kalidas in Sanskrit literature. We consider it very necessary to bring them up to get acquainted with Kalidas' compositions. The following (*shloka*) is popular among Sanskrit scholars:

Kavyeshu natakam ramyam tatra ramyam Shakuntala,
Tatrapi cha chaturthoankastatra shloka chatushtayam.

It means– drama is particularly more appealing among all kinds of poetry. Even among dramas, the name of *Abhigyan Shakuntalam* stands supreme from the viewpoint of poetic beauty. The fourth chapter of *Abhigyan Shakuntalam* is quite tasteful. In that chapter, the fourth verse (*shloka*) is very charming.

Likewise, another scholar has said about Kalidas –

Kalidasgiran saram Kalidassaraswati,
Chaturmukhoathwa brahma vidurnanye tu madrishah.

The means– only three persons have perceived the gist of Kalidas' words so far– the first one is the creator, Brahma, the second one is the goddess of eloquence, Saraswati. The third one is Kalidas himself. Someone like me is unable to comprehend him properly.

An ancient Sanskrit poet has gone further to add.

Kalidas kavita navam vayah maahisham dadhi sasharkaram payah,
Enmasambala sukomala sambhvantu mam janm-janmani.

Its meaning is – I agree to take many births in this world if I am given, Kalidas' verses to read, new, ascending youth, curd made of buffalo's milk, sweetened milk, meat of deer and delicate, young ladies in each birth.

The Indian soul continues to be perpetually restless for emancipation but the poet says that he does not wish emancipation if he gets company of Kalidas' poems along with the other aforesaid things in each birth.

Kalidas has always been introduced along with the *navratnas* of Vikramaditya. His *navratnas* were as follows –

Dhanvantari

He was counted among the nine jewels. Nine treatises, written by him are still available. They are related to Ayurvedic medical science. He was a great expert in the field of medicine.

Kshapanak

He was a Buddhist monk, as is evident from his name. This proves that a ministerial post was not a source of livelihood in the ancient period. Rather, the ministerial cabinet was to be formed keeping the welfare of public in full view. That was the reason why even monks were the members of the ministerial cabinet. He wrote some books out of those *Bhikshaatan* and *Naanaarthhkosha* are available.

Amarsingh

He was a profound scholar. On the basics of a rock inscription found at the present Buddha temple of Bodh Gaya, it has been said that he was the builder of that temple. His name stands tall solely due to *Amarkosh* which is one of the several books he had penned. A saying, which goes popular among Sanskrit scholars, is that *Astadhyaai* is the mother of scholars and *'Amarkosh'* is its father. He who reads the two treatises, becomes a great scholar.

Shanku

His complete name was Shankuk. Only one of his poetic treatises titled *Bhuvanaabhyudayam*, became very famous. He is considered a profound scholar of Sanskrit.

Vetaalbhatt

The stories of Vikram and Vetaal are famous worldwide. It was he who had written *Vetaal Panchvinshati*. However, his name has faded into the oblivion. It has been proved through *Vetal Pachcheesi*, how deeply Vetaalbhatt was influenced by the greatness of emperor Vikram.

Ghatkharpar

His true name was not this. It is a hearsay that he had vowed to fill water with a punctured pitcher at the house of the poet who would beat him in the use of the figures of speech named *anupraas* and *yamak*. Since then only his true name vanished and he became famous by the name of Ghatkharpar. His composition is also titled as *Ghatkharpar Kavyam*. It is a unique book on *anupraas* and *yamak*. This book, *'Neetisaar'* is also available.

Kalidas

It is presumed that Kalidas was the beloved poet of the emperor Vikramaditya. In his books too, he has presented the brighter aspect of the personality of Vikram. Kalidas' story is strange. It is said that he had obtained education due to the blessing of goddess Kali. Therefore, he was given the name Kalidas. It should be *Kaleedas* according to Sanskrit grammar but, acknowledging Kalidas' genius, it was not changed.

However, there are no two opinions about the scholarly and poetic brilliance of Kalidas. Not only he was an outstanding litterateur of his time, but also no litterateur so unique as him has born so far. His four poetic compositions and three dramas are famous. *Shakuntala* is considered to be his best literary composition.

Varahmihir

He has glorified Indian astrology. He has written several books. The prominent among them are – *Brihjjatak*, *Brihaspati Samhitaa*, *Panchsiddhaanti*, *Ganak Taranginee*, *Laghu-Jaatak*, *Samaas Samhitaa*, *Vivaah Patal* etc.

Vararuchi

Like Kalidas, Vararuchi is also reckoned among the foremost poets. *Saduktikarnaamrit*, *Subhashitaavali* and *Shaardandhar Samhitaa* are his creations.

There is a disagreement about his name. There are three persons bearing this name. They are as follows.

1. Commentator of Panineeya Vyakaran – Vararuchi Katyayan.
2. Author of *Prakrit Prakaash* – Vararuchi.
3. The poet found in analects – Vararuchi.

This was a brief introduction of the nine jewels of Vikramaditya.

Shakuntala

Shakuntala was born to Menaka, the celestial damsel, though *rishi* Vishwamitra, whose asceticism (*tapa*) had scared even Indra. He had sent Menaka to the mortal world (*mrityuloka*) to charm the *rishi* and disturb his *tapa*. Soon, a daughter was born to her, Menaka, and she returned to heaven leaving her daughter in the forest. Birds and animals of the forest nursed the girl and when Kanva *rishi*, saw her, he brought her at his *ashram*. Kanva named her as 'Shakuntala' since she was nursed by birds.

Kanva loved her as if she were his own daughter!

The life of Shakuntala has been illustrated in *Abhigyan Shakuntalam*. Several touching episodes have been portrayed in it. One is, at the time, when Dushyant and Shakuntala met for the first time. The second is when Kanva sends off Shakuntala from his *ashram* for her husband's home.

The third episode is when Shakuntala appears in the court of Dushyant and he refuses to recognize her. The fourth episode is when the ring bearing Dushyant's name retrieved by a fisherman is shown to Dushyant. And the fifth episode is that of the union of Dushyant and Shakuntala at the *ashram* of *maharshi* Mareechi.

The popularity of *Abhigyan Shakuntalam* can be estimated by the fact that Sir William Jones translated it in English about 200 years ago in the year 1781. Later, George Forester published the German translation of the English version in the year 1891. The expression of inner feelings, which Gete, the greatest poet of Germany had uttered after reading this translation, is beyond words, he had said.

"If you wish to find the flower of youth and the fruit of mature age and many such materials at one place by which soul is influenced, gets satisfaction and finds succor, that is, if you want to see heaven and mortal world at the same place, I cannot but speak just one name – *Shakuntala*.

Kalidas and Shakespeare are matched in today's literary world. But I consider that this comparison is futile. There is a vast difference between the periods of the two legendary writers. Kalidas is a poet from an ancient period whereas Shakespeare is an author from a relatively recent past. However, regarding old and new, Kalidas has written: "Poetry does not become acceptable for being old. Similarly it can not be rejected for being new."

We are not considering the rejection of Shakespeare's literature for being a recent piece of work. We are only saying that although Shakespeare holds the foremost place in English literature, his comparison with Kalidas' composition can not be proper.

However, if so desired, Tulsidas can be compared with Shakespeare. At one place, Shakespeare has said "The eyes do not have tongue and tongue does not have eyes." But Tulsidas had already expressed this sentiment at the occasion of the first encounter between Rama and Janki at Janakpuri in the following words.

Gira anayan nayan binu baani.

We believe that, after reading it, our valued reader would certainly experience the beauty and amazing uniqueness of Sanskrit poetry and its matchlessness.

- *Ashok Kaushik*

Introduction

Besides being extremely dutiful, emperor Vikramaditya was fond of literature. His ministerial cabinet had such scholars as Kalidas and Bhavbhooti. Recreation of his subject used to be the supreme *dharma* of the king. Emperor Vikramaditya hardly ever missed to do this duty. As a result, different kinds of programmes used to be organized from time to time. These programmes were organized according to season and festival.

Abhigyan Shakuntalam written by Kalidas, was staged on the occasion of one such programme.

Instead of proclaiming through Kalidas' mouth, *sootradhaar* (stage-manager) is employed here to inform that the assembly and the subjects would be entertained by *Abhigyan Shakuntalam* which has been composed by Kalidas.

This is an old tradition of drama. The playwright arranges to deliver his introduction through *sootradhaar* (stage manager) of the drama. Thus, the staging of the drama begins.

Introduction of Characters

Male Characters

Sootradhaar	:	Manager of the drama; introducing character
Dushyant	:	Emperor of Hastinapur, hero of the drama
Bhadrasen	:	Army Commander
Madhavya	:	Jester
Sarvadaman	:	Dushyant's son (Bharat)
Somrat	:	Spiritual *guru* of the king
Raivatak	:	Doorkeeper
Karbhak	:	King's attendant
Parvatayan	:	Chamberlain
Vaitalik	:	King's minstrel
Vaikhanas , Shaaranrav Shardwat, Hareet, and Gautam	]	Disciples of Kanva *rishi*
Shyamal	:	Brother-in-law of king Dushyant, Chief Minister
Dheevar	:	Fisherman
Soochak and Januk	:	Ministers
Mareechi	:	Kashyap (king)
Matali	:	Charioteer of lord Indra
Durwasa	:	A *rishi* (sage)

Female Characters

Natee	:	Wife of *sootradhaar* (manager of the drama)
Shakuntala	:	Foster daughter of Kanva, heroine of the play
Ansooya, Priyamvada	:	Confidante of Shakuntala
Gautami	:	A female ascetic
Chaturika, Parbhritikaa Madhukarikaa	]	Royal attendants
Pratihari, Yavan	:	Chamber maids
Sanumati	:	A celestial damsel
Aditi	:	Kashyap's wife

Contents

Act I

Invocation

Yaa srishtih strashturadya vahati vidhihutam ya havirya cha hotree,
Ye dweykaalamvidhatah shrutivishayagunaha
pranvantah ya sthita vyapya vishvam,
Yamahmahu sarvabeejprakritiriti yaya praninah pranvantah,
Pratyakshabhih prapannstanubhirvatu vartabhirashtabhireeshah.

[The universe which Brahma created first of all, the fire which accepts sacrificial materials offered ritualistically, the sacrificial priest who has been assigned with the job of offering oblation to sacrificial fire, the moon and the sun who determine day and night, the sky whose virtue is word and which pervades the entire universe, the earth which is said to be the origin of all the seeds, and the air due to which all the *jeevs* (living beings) survive, that is, lord Shiv who is visible to all in the eight forms, namely, universe, fire, sacrificial priest, sun, moon, sky, earth, and air may bless you all the beings.]

[Sootradhaar enters]

Sootradhaar : Any further delay is not proper now. (seeing around) *Aarye*, come soon if you are through with your make up.

[Natee enters]

Natee : I have come *Aaryaputra*, at your command! Which play has to be performed today?

Sootradhaar : *Aaryae*, our great king Vikramaditya is a patron of the artistes who create magic of aesthetics and emotions. Besides great scholars are present in his assembly today. Hence, it would be proper to show *Abhigyan Shakuntalam*, to them. It is a new composition of Kalidas. You ask all characters to get ready after adorning their respective costumes and ornaments.

Natee : You have already trained the artistes so much that there is nothing to do for anybody else. Nobody can raise a finger towards them.

Sootradhaar : (with smile) *Aarye*! It is you who is saying this but I do not consider the play successful until the learned persons agree that it is good. Because, in spite of well dressed and trained characters, the mind is not satisfied.

Natee : (humbly) *Aarya*, you are correct; so now, what you command must be made.

Sootradhaar : *Aarye!* Before we carry on our discussion about the play, it would be better to arrange for an interesting song that would delight the ears of the connoisseurs present in the auditorium.

Natee : What type of song should be presented?

Sootradhaar : The summer season is just beginning. It would be good at this time to play a melody in tune with the summer season.

Water during a bath pleases a great deal nowadays. One wants to take bath again and again. The rosy breeze through forest also appeals very much. The dense shadow of trees ends the fatigue and one takes sound sleep under them. Further, evening during these days are charming too.

Natee : Right, so it be. (Begins to sing)

Jin shireesh-sumanon ke sukumaar kesardal ki shikhaayen,
Choom-choomkar rasmaya bhaunrey phir-phir ur baitth-baitth jaayen.
Daya dravit hathhon se chunkar lekar sahridayataa se satvar,
Rachkar karnaphool phir kanon mein pahan rahi pramdayen.

Sootradhaar : *Aarye*! Very melodious song! You sang very beautifully. People are swooning in such a way after listening to your tune that this entire auditorium appears animated. (Pausing a few moments) Which play should be shown to this audience now?

Natee : Hadn't you yourself mentioned a while ago that the audience should be entertained today through the play of the great poet, Kalidas' newly composed drama *Abhigyan Shakuntalam.* Our artists are ready to stage it.

Sootradhaar : Oh yes! I had almost forgotten. You did well to remind me. Actually, your song was so fascinating that its tune captivated my heart as forcefully as ...

[Listens attentively]

This deer, racing fast, has towed king Dushyant here.

[The two depart from the stage]

(End of introduction)

[Sitting on a chariot with charioteer, adorning bow and arrow, chasing the deer, king Dushyant takes entry]

Charioteer : (watching the king and the deer) *Ayushmaan* (blessed with longevity)! With your eyes fixed on this beautiful black deer, and with drawn bowstring, you appear as if a Pinaaki were chasing the deer.

Dushyant : *Soot* (charioteer)! This deer has carried us far off. It is turning back frequently to stare at this chariot. It is scared of my arrow. It keeps on running, shrinking and pulling its hind legs to meet with its forelegs. It is tired of running and therefore, half-chewed straw of sacrificial grass keeps on falling from his mouth on the way. It is taking such long leaps out of fear that its feet do not appear to touch the ground. It seems as if it were running in the sky!

[Showing surprise; seeing around]

Dushyant : We were closely following this deer; how did it disappear from our sight then?

Charioteer : *Ayushmaan*! The ground is very rough and rugged and the chariot was not moving properly. Hence, I had pulled the reins of the horses to slow them down. Running at its usual pace, the deer has gone away from us, it is out of our sight. But the plain ground lies ahead; the chariot will catch speed there and we can capture the deer.

King : That is alright; the plain ground has arrived now. Loosen the reins of the horses so that they could run freely at their speed.

Charioteer : As the *Ayushmaan* commands! (Loosens the reins; seeing the speed of the chariot) *Ayushmaan*!

[Showing the speed of the horses]

As soon as I have loosened the reins, these horses, expanding the forepart of their body and straightening their headstall, are running so fast that the dust rising from their hoofs is unable to touch them. It appears as if these horses are competing with the deer in this race.

King : (pleased) These horses have indeed beaten the horses of the sun and Indra at this moment. The chariot is running so speedily that something is neither away from nor near us.

[After a pause]

Charioteer! Watch out, now I hit this deer.

[The King loads the arrow]

[That very moment, from backstage]

O King! This deer belongs to the hermitage. It should not be killed stop, do not kill it.

Charioteer : (looks around after listening please to with the voice) *Ayushmaan*! The black deer you are aiming at with your arrow is under the protection of hermits.

The King : (worried) Then, pull over the horses.

Charioteer : Right away! (He stops the chariot)

[Vaikhanas enters along with two disciples]

Vaikhanas : (raising hands) King! This deer belongs to our *ashram*. It should not be hunted, for *ashram's* animals are not executable. Deer's body happens to be very soft for which your arrow proves to be as dreadful as fire for a cushion of cotton. Think, on one hand, the tender soul of deer and on the other, your arrows, hard and sharp like *vajra*. Hence, take off the arrow that you have arched. Your weapons should be intended to protect the distressed ones and not to kill the helpless ones.

King : Well, I have taken off my arrow. (Acts on his words after saying so)

Vaikhanas : The progeny of Puru dynasty, this act suits a man like you. Yours appropriate conduct proves that you have taken birth in the Puru dynasty. We pray to God that you get a son of such virtues only as yours.

Both Disciples : (raising their hands) You will have a son, sovereign of the world, by all means.

King : (folding hands) I respectfully accept your blessings.

Vaikhanas : King! Our chancellor *maharshi* Kanva's *ashram* is situated by the river, Malini. We are residents of the *ashram* and have set out to fetch sacrificial sticks from the forest. If you do not have any objection kindly come to the *ashram* and accept our hospitality. There you would see how *rishi*s are performing their piece of work uninterruptedly, you would realize how far your arms, strengthened by the twang of bowstring, are reaching out to protect living creatures.

King : Is the honourable chancellor present there?

Vaikhaanas : He was there a few moments ago. After handing over the charge of hospitality to his delicate daughter Shakuntala, he has departed for *Somteerthha*.

King : Alright, I will meet her. Later, she would inform *maharshiji* how deep reverence I have for *maharshiji*.

Vaikhanas : Yes, that is fine. You go to the *ashram;* we go to pick up the sacrificial sticks.

[Vaikhanas and his disciples depart]

King : Charioteer! Take the chariot towards the *ashram*. Let me sanctify my soul today by visiting this *ashram*.

Charioteer : By the command of A*yushmaan*.

[Charioteer races the chariot speedily]

King : (having a look around) Charioteer! Look. Merely by looking at the milieu around, it comes to mind that we have arrived at the sacred grove of an *ashram*.

Charioteer : How can we conclude this?

King : Are you not seeing all this? The specks of rice, fallen from parrots' nests, are seen dispersed under the trees at some places. Somewhere, smooth stones scattered around are telling that *hingote* fruits have been crushed on them. Somewhere, bold deer are listening delightfully the sounds of our moving chariot. They are confident that even an outsider would not frighten them in any manner in the *ashram*. And see there, the formation of water trail on the approach lane to the river. The water trail shows that we are near a human settlement.

Roots of trees are washed up here by the breeze-induced ripples of water. The colour of buds seems faded due to the smoke of ghee used in *yajna*. Wherever the sacrificial grass has been uprooted from the garden, fawns are grazing the grass, totally unperturbed.

Charioteer : Yes sir, you are right. These things are certainly visible here.

King : Someone is coming near us. Stop the chariot.

Charioteer : I will enquire, *Ayushmaan*.

King : I shall get down and go behind cover.

[The Chariot stops. The king goes behind bushes on the roadside. Watering plants along with her confidantes, Shakuntala enters]

Shakuntala : Compeers! Come here, come here.

Ansooya : *Arye* Shakuntala! I understand that father Kanva loves the trees of this *ashram* even more than you. Otherwise, why should he assign the task of filling the watering can to someone like you who is as delicate as the bud of jasmine?

Shakuntala : I do not irrigate these trees merely because father has assigned this task to me.

Ansooya : What is the reason then?

Shakuntala : I myself love them like my kin and therefore I do all this.

[Shakuntala begins watering the plants]

King : (thinking) Is she the daughter of *maharshi* Kanva? It seems that the great soul, Kanva, is very heartless. He has engaged a delicate maiden like her to do such lowly deeds of the *ashram*. Let it be, I would be watching her from this shelter as long as she waters plants.

[Keeps on looking at Shakuntala from behind the bush]

Shakuntala : Compeer Ansooya! Priyambada has fastened my garment (*valkal*) so tight that I find it difficult to carry on with my work. Come and loosen it a bit.

Ansooya : Alright.

[Ansooya loosens the *Valkal*]

Priyambada : (laughing) Why do you reproach me? Why don't you complain to your youth that keeps on expanding your bosoms like this?

King : (thinking) Although her delicate body is not suitable to wear *valkal* (garment made of bark), it decorates her body just like ornaments.

[The king comes from behind the bush and rides the chariot. The Charioteer prompts the horses to move forward]

King : The sacred grove dwellers must not have any inconvenience due to the chariot moving any closer. Hence, we should halt the chariot here only. I will get down right here. Moving on foot from here onwards would be more suitable.

[Charioteer halts the chariot just outside the main gate of the *ashram*]

Charioteer : *Ayushmaan* may get down now.

[The king descends from the chariot]

King : Charioteer! It would be apt to visit an *ashram* attired as a common man. I must take off my ornaments etc. right here.

[The king takes puts off his ornaments etc. along with bow-arrow and hands them over to the charioteer]

King : Look Charioteer! You let loose the horses and allow them to take them rest until I return, after meeting with the *ashram* dwellers.

Charioteer : Very well, sir.

[The king departs towards the ashram]

King : (advances ahead; talks to himself) This seems to be the ashram's door.

[The King enters through the door. He observes some good omens]

King : (thinking) Why is my right eye fluttering? What can a king like me possibly get here at this *ashram?* It has been said that what has to happen can occur anywhere.

[In the background]

Compeers! Come here, come here.

[The King listens attentively]

King : (to himself) The sound of conversation seems to be coming from the right side of the small flower-garden. (looking around) Aha! These daughters of hermits, carrying pitchers, are coming to this direction to water small plants. (looking carefully) Oh! As lotus appears beautiful in spite of being surrounded by swamp and the blemish attached with the moon only enhances its splendour, this *valkal* – adorning beauty looks very attractive. In fact, any thing would be fire on her beautiful body.

Shakuntala : (looking in front) Look, this saffron tree is calling me with its leaves as if they were fingers, swaying with the rush of wind!

[Turns towards it after saying this]

Priyambada : *Hey* Shakuntala! Wait for a moment right there. When you stand with this tree, this saffron tree appears as if some vine were coiled around it!

Shakuntala : Since you talk like this, you have got the name Priyambada.

King : (to himself) Priyambada has told her confidante a total truth. Her red lips appear as shoots of vine. The two arms seem like delicate branches. And the youth that has bloomed in every part of her body fascinates me like a beautiful flower.

Ansooya : Shakuntala! Isn't it the same new jasmine which was married off to the mango tree. You had given her the name, *Van-Jyotsana.* Aren't you forgetting her?

Shakuntala : Wow! How can that happen! I shall never forget that.

[Shakuntala goes near the vine and inspects it]

Shakuntala : Compeer! Indeed this vine and the tree have met during a very auspicious time. On the one hand, this *'Van-Jyotsana'* has acquired new youth due to the blooming flowers, on the other hand the mango tree, with its branches bearing fruits, is on its full youth.

[Continues to stand and watch both the tree and vine]

Priyambada : (smiling) Ansooya! Do you know why is Shakuntala watching this *'Van-Jyotsana'* so intently?

Ansooya : No confidante! At least I do not know. Do tell why she is being so engrossed.

Priyambada : She is contemplating how nice it would be if she could find a suitable groom for herself just like this *'Van-Jyotsana'* has clung to a tree worthy of it.

Shakuntala : (blushes) Don't speak like that; I feel ashamed.

[Waters the tree with the water pitcher]

King : (thinking) Hasn't this daughter of a *rishi* taken birth from a woman of some other caste? But why should one doubt? When a pure heart like mine has begun to desire her, it is certain that this maiden can marry a *kshatriya*. Because when in doubt, gentlemen should accept what their mind approves. Whatever be, I shall try to know the right details from her.

Shakuntala : (vexed) Upset by the drizzle of water falling on its body, this flying blackbee is hovering around my face instead of the jasmine.

[Acts as if aggrieved by the blackbee]

King : (as if yearning, thinks) *Hey* blackbee! You are truly very fortunate, for you are being watched by her restless glance. You are touching this trembling young woman again and again, humming slowly close to her ears as trying to tell her a major secret. And, in spite of being pushed away by her hands, you continue to drink the nectar of her juicy lips. On the other side, it is I who have lost my real objective - getting the correct information about her.

Shakuntala : Oh! This wicked blackbee does not give up. Must leave this spot and go to other place.

[Going to another spot and glancing to the other side]

Shakuntala : Oh! Has it come here too? What should I do now? Friends! Save, me from this wicked blackbee. It has troubled me a lot.

Both : (smiling) Who are we to save you? And why don't you call for king Dushyant? It is king's duty to protect this sacred grove.

King : (thinking) Do not be scared, do not be scared. She must know now that I am the king.

Shakuntala : (goes forward to cover a little distance and then turns to look back at the blackbee) What to do? It is not leaving the chase even here.

King : (appears out of hiding suddenly.) Oh! Who is it that dares to harass these delicate hermit girls as long as the punisher of evil, the descendant of the Puru dynasty, is ruling this earth?

[The three are startled upon seeing the king]

Ansooya : *Arya*! It is not a major trouble. A blackbee has harassed our dear confidante. Therefore, she was worried a bit.

[Points towards Shakuntala after saying this]

King : (moves to face Shakuntala) I hope that blackbee is not bothering you any longer. Is it?

[Shakuntala keeps quiet with her face downwards]

Ansooya : The arrival of a special guest at this time calls for quick actions. (addresses Shakuntala) Shakuntala! Proceed to the cottage and bring some fruits along with potable water. The water for washing the guest's feet is available here.

King : My hospitality has been completed by your sweet words.

Priyambada : *Arya*! Then move and sit upon the cool platform under the densely shadowed *Saptvarnee* forest. Take rest there only.

King : All of you must have become tired of working.

Priyambada : Shakuntala! Now, we must honour the suggestion of the guest. Come, let us take rest by sitting here.

[Thus, all sit down]

Shukuntala : (thinking) Don't know, why a strange kind of upheaval is occurring in my mind upon seeing this person. Sacred grove's dwellers should not nurture such feelings.

King : (looking at all) All you are of same age and equally attractive beauties. Your mutual cordiality seems to be very charming.

Priyambada : (in low voice) Ansooya! This astute and profound-looking person speaks very sweet. Perhaps, he is a prominent person.

Ansooya : (to Priyambada in low voice) Confidante! I am curious to know. Let us ask him.

Ansooya : (overtly) *Arya*, our trust in you that has developed due to your sweet talk is compelling us to ask you which royal family the *Arya* has graced? Also, may I humbly ask – for what purpose *Arya* has arrived at the sacred grove?

Shakuntala : (thinking) Oh heart! Do not become so impatient. After all Ansooya is asking the same that is in your mind.

King : (thinking) How to introduce myself and how to conceal my identity? (overtly) Noble ladies! Pururaj Dushyant has given me the responsibility to oversee the religious activities of his kingdom. Therefore, I have come to supervise and find out if there is any interruption in the activities of the *ashram's* ascetics.

Ansooya : *Arya*! You have done a great favour to the folks engaged in religious activities.

[Shakuntala blushes]

Both : (noticing the internal feelings of Shakuntala and Dushyant, speak slowly) Shakuntala! Only if father was home today, what would happen?

Shakuntala : What would happen then?

Both : He would have satisfied this special guest offering his whole possession of life.

Shakuntala : Move away, you two! You blurt out whatever visits your mind. Now, I will not even listen to your words.

King : (to the two compeers) I also wish to ask something about your confidante.

Compeers : *Arya*! Ask, what do you want to ask?

King : The whole world has known so far that Lord Kanva has been celibate since birth. Then, how did this confidante of yours become his daughter?

Ansooya : Listen *Arya*! I can tell you. A very great *rajrishi* happened to be in a *gotra* (family) named Kaushik.

King : Yes, it is true. I have heard about him.

Ansooya : *Rishi* Kaushik is father of our confidante. Her mother had deserted her. *Maharshi* Kanva has grown her up; hence, she calls him as her father.

King : My curiosity is flaring up even more after listening about desertion by her mother. I express my wish to listen her whole story.

Ansooya : *Arya*! Listen. Very long ago, *raajarshi* Kaushik was absorbed in deep austerity at the banks of river Gomti. It is a hearsay that, envied by his penance, gods sent a celestial damsel to him to disturb him.

King : Well, I have also heard this fable gods do get scared upon seeing other sages' austerity.

Ansooya : So, upon seeing her intoxicating youth in the season of spring ...

[Blushes to continue further and stops]

King : No need to say any further; it can be guessed. This confidante of yours is truly a daughter of a celestial damsel.

Ansooya : Why not?

King : Otherwise, where does one find such a beauty among humans? Seductive, shining, lightning... She did not emerge from the earth!

[Shakuntala stoops her head]

King : (thinking) Well, my wish got fulfilled to some extent but her compeer, Priyambada, had been talking in amusement about her fiancé. This develops doubt in my mind, lest she should be already engaged.

Priyambada : (smiles and glances towards Shakuntala first and towards the king afterwards) *Arya*! Do you wish to enquire anything else?

[Shakuntala admonishes her with her finger]

King : You have guessed my mind. Hungry to hear her pleasing story, I wish to ask something more.

Priyambada : What are you thinking then? You can ask anything from hermits without any hitch.

King : I want to know regarding your confidante about would she spend the hermit-like attire, which she has adorned. It is causing obstruction to the force of *Kaamdev* (Cupid). Would she spend her whole life among deer, or would she ever get married?

Priyambada : *Arya*! The poor fellow is dependent even for religious acts. Still, our *guruji* has resolved to get her married to a suitable groom, if one is found.

King : (thinking) The fulfillment of this prayer is not difficult. So, do not leave hope. Now, the doubt has been cleared.

Shakuntala : (expressing displeasure) I am parting.

Ansooya : Why? What are you going away for?

Shakuntala : I want to inform *aryaa* Gautami about this kind of rigmarole voiced by Priyambada.

Ansooya : Compeer! Your departure in this fashion without extending hospitality towards such a prominent guest is not proper.

[Shakuntala prepares to go without responding to her]

King : (thinking) Why are you leaving?

[King rises to stop her but then holds himself] I was going to follow this *muni* maiden but have stopped myself out of modesty.

Priyambada : (intercepting Shakuntala) Confidante! Your departure in this fashion is not proper.

Shakuntala : (raising her eyebrows) Why is it not proper?

Priyambada : Because you have just lost a bet to me for which you have yet to water two trees. First, clear your debt. Then, you can go but not before that.

King : (to Priyambada) Noble lady! Since she has been watering plants appears to be tired. Her shoulders have been bent by lifting pitchers. Her palms have turned red, her heaving bosoms tell that she is out of breath due to exhaustion. Even *siras* flowers worn on ears are not moving because their petals have stuck to her cheeks due to drops of perspiration. As her hair-do has loosened, she is putting in great effort to handle her disheveled locks of hair with her one hand. Now, it is difficult for her to repay the debt; well I repay her debt.

[King wants to offer his ring. Both the confidantes begin to look at each other after reading the name of Dushyant inscribed on the ring]

King : Do not misunderstand me for someone else. Actually, I have received this ring as reward from the king. Consider me a royal servant only, nothing else.

Priyambada : Then, you should not part this ring from your finger. You have said that you have to pay the debt. Treat my confidante's debt cleared merely by this gesture of yours. Shakuntala, you are free from debt by his, or say the king's kindness. You can go if you wish so.

Shakuntala : (thinking) I can go only if my mind is under my control. (overtly) Who are you to let me go or stop?

King : (thinking and seeing Shakuntala) Isn't so that she is also charmed by me, just like I am charmed by her. Or, it seems that days of fructification of my desires have arrived. Although she does not talk to me herself, she listens to my talk intently whenever I speak. Further, she does not face me but her eyes keep gazing at me.

[In the background]

Hey hermits! Come and save the creatures of the sacred grove. King Dushyant, fond of hunting, has arrived. The red dust, like the ruddiness of the evening, taking off from the hoofs of his horses is falling on those trees of the *ashram* on whose branches wet *valkal* garments are hanging.

Look again! Afraid of the king's chariot, this wild elephant, a real trouble for our sages, scattering the flock of deer, is trespassing this sacred grove. It has uprooted a tree. The severed vines of the tree, have also stuck in its legs.

[All are worried listening to this]

King : (internally) Curse on my soldiers. It seems that these soldiers are trampling the sacred grove even as they search for me. I must follow them.

Both : *Arya*! We are scared to hear about this wild elephant. Now permit us to return to the cottage.

King : (hurriedly) Please proceed. I shall make efforts to ensure that no disturbance takes place in the sacred grove.

Both : *Arya*! We have extended no hospitality towards you, therefore (all the three get up) we feel sorry. We request you to oblige us by visiting us again.

King : Do not say so. This was a divine meeting.

[Shakuntala, pretending to be pinched by the sacrificial grass and tangled into a branch, halts for a moment to behold the king and then goes off with compeers]

King : The keenness to return to the city has faded. Therefore, I should camp along with the soldiers near the *ashram*. It looks as if I will not get freedom from this loving behaviour of Shakuntala.

[All depart]

●

Act II

[Jester enters with a heavy heart and a sullen face]

Jester : (breathes deep) Just enough. My heart is worried on account of friendship with the king, who is fond of hunting. When it is time to relax in the middle of the noon, wandering from one jungle to another, I have to pass through such wild places where even leaves do not quiver due to heat. Therefore, I find no place to relax. My soldiers keep on informing me thus. Look here comes a deer. The boar just dipped away. Look there! It is a lion. And then, I have to drink the bitter water from the rivers overflowing with rotten leaves. The meat roasted on iron bars is given to me. Running behind the horses, all the joints of my body have loosened, so I cannot even sleep properly. Above all, these bird catchers make such a din. They say, move to jungle in the morning, move to jungle in the morning, so, my early-morning sleep is disturbed. I hear that, having lost our company and while, chasing a deer, the king has also reached at an *ashram* of hermits. And to my misfortune, *muni* maiden, Shakuntala, has met him. Now, by no means, he desires to return to the city. Even today, his eyes didn't wink for a minute throughout the whole night, as he kept thinking about her. What should I do? Let me go and see; I shall talk to him a few words if he is done with his morning chores.

(Turns around and looks) *Ahah!* It is my friend; he is coming in this direction and accompanying him are so many *yavani* maid-assistants, with bow-arrow in hands and adorned with garlands, made of wild flowers.

[Rises to stand with the support of a stick]

[King enters with the same type of maid-assistants as jester had narrated]

King : Although it is extremely difficult to meet dear Shakuntala, my mind has got assurance through the expression of her disposition. Even if the union of us may not occur, the matter of consolation is that the craving to unite is equally strong on both the sides.

(smiling) A lover who evaluates his beloved's mind with his own, gets deceived like this.

When she turned her eyes lovingly towards someone else, I used to think that she had thrown her loving glance towards me only. When she walked with slow gait due to her heavy hips, I used to think that she was parading her ostentatious steps. The way she became angry with her compeers when they prevented her from going away on some pretext, I thought that was happening due to her love towards me. Ahoy! A lustful person visualizes everything so rosy, so romantic!

Jester : My hands and feet are not moving, therefore, I hail you verbally. Victory to you, O king!

King : How did you become crippled?

Jester : What do you mean by 'how?' Having poked your finger in my eyes, you are enquiring about tears?

King : I am unable to understand what you are saying. Be candid, what is the matter?

Jester : My friend! Well, now explain to me, does the bamboo creeper, which flows with the river and appears hunched, become so on its own, or it becomes so due to the force of the river?

King : It has to acquire that shape due to the force of the river.

Jester : Then, it is you only who is the reason behind my mutilation.

King : How could that be?

Jester : Shirking your stately duties, you are roaming in this rugged terrain like a wild creature, whereas, chasing wild animals, my body joints have broken in such a way that I cannot even move. Now, be kind and allow me to relax at least for one day.

King : (thinking) On one side, he too is talking of retiring and on the other, I have seemingly lost charm for hunting thinking over *maharshi* Kanva's daughter. I am helpless to load a single arrow on the bow to kill those deer that, in the company of Shakuntala, have taught me to throw innocent glances. Arching the bowstring is difficult for me even if I load the arrow.

Jester : (observing the King's face) I don't know. What you are murmuring to yourself? Was I talking to jungle so far?

King : (smiling) It is not so. I have heard you carefully. I was also mulling over that. I should not ignore the suggestion of a friend. Hence, I had become silent of sorts.

Jester : May you live for ages. (tries to go after saying this)

King : Friend! Wait for a moment. I have not completed my sentence yet.

Jester : Great King! Please command. What do you want to say?

King : Come to me after you have completed your relaxation. I need your assistance for one task. Be assured, you would not have to go anywhere for that job.

Jester : Do I have to eat *laddu* (sweetmeat) then? What could be a better occasion for that than this one?

King : Wait, tell you right away. (calls out) Hey! Is there anyone here?

Doorkeeper : (comes and bows before the King) *Swami!* Please command.

King : Raivtak! You do this little job and send for army commander.

Doorkeeper : At your command great King!

[Doorkeeper goes out and returns, accompanying the army commander]

Army commander : (thinking) People term hunting as unworthy but its visible demerits have only benefited our *swami*. Like the elephant wandering in mountains, the front part of his strong body has hardened so much by continuously pulling on the arch that it is neither affected by sunshine nor rain. Although he has become lean due to excessive running around in jungles, his emaciated physique is sturdy, strong and capable of withstanding any crises – physical or mental.

(on going near; covertly) Victory to *swami*. We have seized the games in the forest. What is the delay then?

King : Madhavya, he is the detractor of hunting. He has demoralized my zeal.

Army commander : (talking separately to the jester) Well! So, did you cause him to change mind? Alright friend! You decry hunting with full steam and see how I reverse the decision of my *swami*. (overtly) Great King! Let this fool babble. *Swami*! You are noticing yourself that one's fat is reduced due to hunting; tummy recedes; one's body becomes light and agile. One learns about the fright and ferocity that appears on the face of the animals when one hunts them. Also, one's hands acquire expertise to aim at the moving target, which is a matter of great pride for archers. People unnecessarily criticize hunting. It is the best method of recreation and hard-core learning.

Jester : *Hey*, move away, move away from here. Can't you see that our great King has become a human once again? Straying from one jungle to another and hunting like this, you have to go into the mouth of a large bear.

King : Noble Army Commander! See, we have camped near the sacred grove at present. Therefore, at this time, I do not appreciate you to go on hunting. Release the buffaloes so that they may be able to swim in the ponds. Flocks of deer could sit in the circles under the shadow of the trees and ruminate. The large boars can go fearlessly into shallow ponds and dig out the roots of cyprus (sweet smelling grass). Besides, the loose string of my bow would also relax for a while.

Army Commander : As the great king may deem proper.

King : Recall the drummers who have gone ahead. Also instruct your entire army that they should not do any such action which might create any hindrance in the activities of the sacred grove.

Although *rishis* happen to be very calm, they have such radiance that they can turn every thing, that troubles them into ash.

Army Commander : As per the command of *swami*. I will recall the drummers right away.

Jester : To hell with your talks of zeal.

[The Army Commander departs]

King : (looking towards his attendants) Now, you all take off your hunter's attire. Noticing Raivtak, Yes Raivtak! You also do your job.

Raivtak : As my master commands.

[All depart]

Jester : You have done well to drive off all these flies from here. Now, walk out from here. Proceed and sit on the pleasant seat under the arbour surrounded by deep shadow of trees. I shall also remove my fatigue. My whole body is languid.

King : You move ahead.

Jester : I am moving; you come too.

[Both sit opposite each other]

King : Madhavya! What is the use of these eyes of yours if you did not see the objects worth seeing?

Jester : Don't you always live before my eyes?

King : Everybody considers himself attractive. But I was talking about Shakuntala who is the real grace of this *ashram*.

Jester : (thinking) Well, now I know. I cut this topic short. (overtly) Well friend! It seems that you have been attracted towards that hermit maiden.

King : Friend! The mind of the Puru clan cannot go on a wrong course.

I have learnt that her mother was a celestial damsel. When she deserted her in the forest after her birth, *muni* Kanva brought her here.

Jester : (amused) One, after getting bored of eating sweet dates, pounces upon tamarind. In the same way, you too have been charmed by her bewitching beauty. You have ignored all other beauties of your *antahpur* (harem) and are after this damsel of the grove.

King : You are saying so because you have not seen her even once yet.

Jester : It is quite understandable. She must be truly beautiful, no doubt. That is why you have lost your senses after seeing her.

King : What can I say to you? You only understand in nutshell that Brahma must have created her image first before creating her. Or, he must have created in his mind the images of all beauties of the world and then, he must have infused life to their collective beauty. He has created a unique beauty.

Jester : If that is so, then she has beaten all other beauties.

King : Her beauty is as pure as a flower which has not been sniffed. She is a flower untouched by thorns. She is fresh, divine honey that hasn't been tasted. She is the result of good deeds *(punya)* that has not been used. I am unable to figure out for who Lord Brahma may have created her.

Jester : If that is the matter, you grab this opportunity promptly so that she does not fall into the hands of some other hermit.

King : But the poor girl is dependent; getting married to a man of her dreams is not under her control. And her father, the holy sage is not present here.

Jester : Alright! Then tell me, what had happened to her when she glanced at you?

King : Friend! Hermit maidens happen to be very innocent by nature. She also avoided meeting my eyes with hers. Nevertheless, she would smile on one or the other pretext, whenever I turned my face towards her. She seemed to be so subdued due to modesty that she was neither able to conceal her love nor able to express it openly.

Jester : (laughing) Should she come and sit in your lap then?

King : What nonsense are you talking? Listen, when she was departing, she expressed her love despite all the controls of the grove. After covering ahead by a few steps, the beauty suddenly stopped and said, "Oh! A thorn of rope has pierced my feet." Although her *valkal* had not been tangled anywhere, she stood there for some time looking towards me, pretending to disentangle her *valkal* slowly.

Jester : Then, you better bring your entire paraphernalia here only. I can see that you have begun to treat this sacred grove as an entertainment grove.

King : Friend! Some native *rishi*s have identified me. Now tell me some way so that my entry to the *ashram* may become easy on some pretext at least once.

Jester : *Wah*, you are a king and the King may does not need any pretext for his actions. You can go straight and say that you are the king and that you have arrived in this forest with the desire to collect royal tax as the sixth part of the *neevakaran* that *rishis* collect.

King : Madhavya! You are completely foolish. Should I go and talk of tax collection from *rishi*s? My dear, we receive such a unique tax in exchange of the protection of these *rishi*s that a heap of gems is a trifle in front of it.

The effect of the tax that kings get from the twelve castes (*varna*s) ends after the lapse of some time but one sixth part of the austerity that these *rishi*s, who practice austerity living in the forest, provide us in the form of tax is most valuable.

[In the background]

Unknown voices : Aha, all of our tasks have been accomplished.

King : (listens attentively) H*ey*, such a profound and composed voice could belong to hermits only.

Doorkeeper : (after making entry) Victory to great King. Great King! Two young *rishi*s are waiting at the door.

King : Respectfully usher them here immediately.

Doorkeeper : I shall usher them in right away.

[He goes out. After a while, he enters alongwith two young *rishi*s]

Come deities! Come here.

[Both look at the king]

First *Rishi* : *Ahoy*! He is so bright that his trustworthiness manifests itself on his face. We feel safe and assured after seeing him.

After all the King also lives like *rishi*s. The *rishi* folks live in *ashrams*. He has come to this *ashram* to please us. Thus, he also observes a kind of austerity by dedicating himself to the protection of his state subject.

Second *Rishi* : Gautam! Is that he, the friend of Indra, King Dushyant?

First *Rishi* : Of course, yes.

Second *Rishi* : I am not surprised to learn that, with his large and well-built arms, he rules the entire earth all by himself. The divine maidens, unlike the wily demons, hope of victory on his stretched bow and Indra's weapon (*vajra*).

Both *Rishis* : (going near the king) Great King! May you be victorious!

King : (rises from his seat) I pay my obeisance to both of you.

Both : May you prosper, (offer fruits to the king after giving blessings.

King : (respectfully accepts the fruits) Give me order, please.

Both : All the *ashram* dwellers have come to know that you have camped here. They have pleaded you ...

King : (interrupting in the middle) What is their command?

Both : Demons are causing disruption in our *yajna* due to absence of our chancellor revered *maharshi* Kanva from the *ashram*. Therefore, we entreat you to stay in this *ashram* along with your charioteer and others for a few nights and kindly extend your patronage to us.

King : I am highly obliged.

Jester : (addressing to no one) Their entreaty is favourable to you at this time. You wanted this only.

King : (smiling) Raivatak! Tell the charioteer at my behest to bring the chariot with bow and arrows here.

Doorkeeper : By the command of the great king.

[Departs]

Both *Rishi*s : (expressing happiness) You are doing the same logical job that your ancestors have been doing in the past. It is indeed your *dharma* to protect this *ashram*. It is well known that the clan of the Purus never refuses to protect those who seek protection from its kings.

King : (after folding hands) You both proceed. I shall follow you.

Both : (blessing) May you be victorious!

[Both depart]

King : Madhavya! Do you have any desire to see Shakuntala?

Madhavya : Earlier, when you had mentioned about her, the desire was very overpowering. But since I have heard about the nuisance of demons not an iota of the desire is left anymore.

King : Why are you afraid? I will keep you close to me.

Jester : Alright, then I shall remain protected from demons.

[Doorkeeper enters]

Doorkeeper : Great king! The chariot is ready. It is waiting to tread your victory path. Karbhak has also come from the city after getting permission from the queen mother.

King : (expressing respect for queen mother) Has the queen mother sent Karbhak?

Doorkeeper : Yes sir.

King : Then send him here right away.

[Doorkeeper departs and enters with Karbhak]

Doorkeeper : (to Karbhak) The great king is seated here; please go ahead.

Karbhak : Victory to great king. Revered mother has sent the message that the finale of her fast will fall on the fourth day from today. Her son must be present there on that occasion.

King : On this side, the task of hermits and on the other one the command of the queen mother. Neither of the two tasks can be postponed. What should I do?

Jester : Hang yourself in the middle, like Trishanku.

King : Truly, I have been caught in a dilemma. The two tasks are to be executed at two different places. Hence, in this confusion, the state of my mind is the same as that of a river which is obstructed by a mountain. (Having thought something) Friend! See, revered mother considers you like her son. Therefore, you return to the city and explain to mother that I am engaged in the task of protecting these *rishi*s at present. You would do whatever is there to do for a son.

Jester : Don't think I am afraid of demons.

King : (smiling) Can it ever be thought about you?

Jester : Then, I will go in the same way as King's younger brother ought to go.

King : Alright. As far as possible, all these complications should be kept away from the sacred grove. Therefore, I am sending back the entire army along with you.

Jester : Then, I have virtually become a prince!

King : (thinking) This brahmin is very mischievous. He would go to queen's palace and narrate full details that happened here in the context of my meeting with Shakuntala. I should try to explain (overtly, holding the hand of the jester) Friend! I give great respect to *rishi*s. I have become ready to live in their *ashram* because these *rishi*s are very knowledgeable and revered. The discussion about the *rishi* maiden was useless; I have no love in my heart for her. Where do we royal folks stand and where does the *rishi* maiden stand? She is totally ignorant of the love affair. Friend! Do not treat all this talk as true; I have been telling you all this jokingly.

Jester : Yes, I understand.

[All depart]

•

Act III

[Entry of *yajman* (householder who performs the sacrifice through priest) disciple with sacrificial grass in his hand]

Disciple : See the heroism of the great king, Dushyant, because all our tasks are being accomplished without any hindrance since the time he has arrived at the *ashram*. He removes all our troubles merely by the twang of his bowstring and the roaring of Indra's *vajra*. He need not use arrows to take care of your woes. So, I should proceed and deliver this mattress for spreading at the *yajna* altar, to him. It is meant for the *ritvijas.*

[In the background]

O Priyambada! For who, are you taking this paste made of stemmed lotus leaf and *khas* (scented root of a grass)?

[Again from the background]

What did you say? Is Shakuntala feeling very uneasy because she has caught sunstroke? Are you taking this thing to bring succor to her body? Then go at once. She is like the breath of our chancellor, through Lord Kanva. Meanwhile, I shall also go and arrange to send water through Gautami.

[Departs]

[Curtain drops]

[Entry of the King, restless with lust]

King : (worried and breathing hard) I am very well aware of the power of hermits. Therefore, I cannot even abduct my beloved; besides, I also know that getting married is not in the control of the maiden. She is a dependent person. Hence, she cannot go along with me on her own. In spite of that, I don't know why I am unable to shift my attention away from her.

[Experiencing the affliction of lust]

O Lord of lust *(Kaamdeva)* who adorns floral weapons! With the help of the moon, you have committed great treachery with all those love-bitten people who had put their faith in you.

I am separated from my beloved. It seems as if the moon were raining fire through its cool rays! You too have packed your floral arrows with the hardness of *vajra*, O lord of lust!

She has intoxicating and large eyes. They hurt my soul for they are so beautiful. You are doing the right thing.

[After going around regretfully]

Where would I take my saddened spirit and recreate my mind when these *rishi*s would send me off after the completion of *yajna*? Till then, I have to search for her.

[Heaves a sigh]

Where else is my refuge, except the sight of my beloved? I shall proceed and search for her.

[Seeing towards the sun]

Shakuntala along with her confidantes often sits at the arbour along the banks of river Malini in the afternoons. Well, I had better go there and look for her there itself.

[Turns and acts as if touched by the wind]

Aah! What a pleasant breeze is blowing here.

Steeped with the scent of lotus and saturated with the fountains of Malini's waves, this wind seems to be very pleasant to body that is feverish due to lust.

[Looks around]

Shakuntala must be sitting somewhere in this arbour surrounded by vines.

[Looking below]

These fresh footprints belongs to her heavy-hipped compeers. They are deep towards the heel and shallow towards the toe. They are visible on the yellow sand. Well, I sneak from the cover of these trees.

[Turns around and becomes happy]

Wow! My eyes have found solace. My beloved is lying here, on a stone platform that has been converted into a beautiful floral bed. Both her compeers are engaged in her service. Well, let me hear what kind of discussion is going on among them?

[Listens]

[Change of scene]

[Shakuntala and her compeers appear on the scene in the same state as narrated above by the king]

King : Shakuntala appears like very ill.

[Thinking]

Is she afflicted with sunstroke? Or, is it possible that she is having the same state of mind as mine?

[Looks wistfully]

But why should there be any doubt?

I can see that *khas* paste has been applied on her bosoms; a loose bracelet made of lotus stalk is wrapped around her on one hand. Although she is so restless, her body appears no less attractive even in this state. Although the fever of sunstroke and love lead to the same uneasiness, These maidens do not retain their original beauty upon being afflicted by sunstroke.

Priyamvada : (separately) Ansooya! Since Shakuntala has seen the *rajarshi,* she has been attracted towards him. It might be possible that her fever is due to that infatuation.

Ansooya : Compeer! Even I have a similar doubt in my mind. Alright. Why should we not enquire from her then?

[Openly]

Confidante! We want to ask you about something. See, your anguish has been growing steadily.

Shakuntala : (half-lying on the bed) Compeer! What is it?

Ansooya : Shakuntala! We do not know anything about love. Even then your condition appears to be something like what we have read and heard about lovers in the historical stories. Now you tell us what is the cause of your agony? How is remedy possible until the disease is diagnosed appropriately?

King : (thinking) Her confidante Ansooya is thinking the same that I had thought. It means that my thoughts were not merely too imagination.

Shakuntala : (thinking) In fact, my love has gone too far. Even then, I am unable to utter a word about to them.

Priyambada : Shakuntala! Ansooya is right. Why are you causing your illness to grow in this manner? You are getting emaciated by the day. Just a shade of beautiful lovely appearance has remained on your body.

King : (thinking) Priyambada is telling the truth. Her tender cheeks have withered; mouth has dried. The firmness of bosoms has also disappeared. Her waist has become thin even further. Her shoulders have stooped on and her entire body has turned pale. She has become such due to cupid.

Shakuntala : Who would I confide in if I would not say to you? Confidante! Both of you must do something for me now. Nobody else can be given this trouble.

Both : *Hey*, that is why we both have been insisting for so long. By sharing one's sorrow with soul mates, one assuages its agony to some extent, so it becomes bearable.

King : (listening to them and thinking) This young woman would certainly disclose her heart's secret on being asked by these all-weather friends of hers. Although Shakuntala had glanced at me frequently, lovingly and longingly, at that time my heart is palpitating. Let me see, what she narrates to her compeers regarding her anguish.

Shakuntala : Confidante! Since the time that *rajarshi*, the protector of this *ashram*, has met me. I have been under to this condition.

King : (joyfully but thinking) That is what I wanted to hear! The *kaamdev* (Cupid) who was tormenting me, has breathed life into me.

Shakuntala : If both of you deem it fit, do something so that the *rajarshi* may bestow on me his kindness. Otherwise, consider my death near. You all get prepared to abandon me.

King : All my doubts have vanished after listening to this!

Priyambada : (taking Ansooya aside) Confidante! Her love story has gone so far that something must be done about it soon. She has chosen the great King, Dushyant, the Jewel of Puru dynasty. Her choice must be appreciated.

Ansooya : Yes, indeed!

Priyambada : (openly) Confidante! You are very fortunate because such a worthy man has attracted your attention. Tell me, where else would a great river go except a mighty ocean? Where else the creeper of fragrant flower with new leaves would go for shelter except the mango tree?

King : No wonder if both the stars of *Vishakha* follow the sixteen phases of the moon.

Ansooya : Then, find out a solution by which my confidante's wish gets fulfilled at once and no body could get an inkling of it.

Priyambada : The solution for immediate wish fulfillment is at hand. But contemplation is required to ensure that is not made known to the *rajarshi* of it.

Ansooya : Why?

Priyambada : The *rajarshi* has started loving Shakuntala as much Shakuntala loves him. Therefore, he also looks frail and melancholic since he has been keeping awake for nights and days.

King : My condition has actually become so. I have become so gaunt that this gold armlet, fastened on my arm and supporting my head, has become loose, being sullied due to warm tears trickling from the corners of my eyes.

Priyambada : (after thinking something) Confidante! In this situation, we should make her write a love letter. Concealed under flowers, the love letter should be delivered to the king under the guise of God's ambrosia.

Ansooya : This is a good suggestion. But what is Shakuntala's opinion about it? Let us ask her too.

Shakuntala : It is beyond my capacity to mend your ideas.

Priyambada : Then, you create a beautiful poem, narrating your condition, for that love letter.

Shakuntala : I would write the poem but my heart trembles by the mere thought of writing it. What would happen if he refused to reciprocate?

King : (joyfully and thinking) He himself is very keen to meet you and you are apprehensive of rejection.

Both Confidantes : *Hey*, why do you think about yourself in such a manner? Just cheer up! Who would be such a fool who would cover himself under a canopy to skip absorbing the moonlight that gives solace to him?

Shakuntala : (smiling) Alright, I willl do as you say.

[Shakuntala is sitting and contemplates]

King : This is an excellent opportunity to watch my beloved. As her raised eyebrows like vines, cheeks thrilled with joy and entire body trembling with the excitement of love tells me how deeply she loves me.

Shakuntala : Confidante! I have already contemplated what I should write in the poem. But how to write? There is no writing material with us.

Priyambada : Use your nails as pen and ink and you write on this lotus leaf which is extremely soft as a parrot's chest.

Shakuntala : (doing accordingly)

[After writing]

Shakuntala : Confidante! I have written. Now, you listen to it once whether the poem has been a fine piece of work.

Both compeers : Yes, you recite; we are listening.

Shakuntala : (begins to recite)

Don't know
The secret of your heart,
But
O heartless,
Ensnared by your love,
I writhe in pain,
Night and day!

King : (suddenly comes forward) Cupid (*kaamdev*) is merely disturbing you but it has been persistently burning me. That is because water lily does not wither so much after daybreak as and when the moon declines.

Compeers : (delightfully) You are welcome! We were just thinking about you and our wish has been fulfilled at once.

[Shakuntala wants to get up]

King : Don't get up. The flower petals have stuck to your body due to the perspiration while you turned over on the floral bed. So, you too were afflicted with the fever of separation. The ornaments made of lotus stem, which you have adorned, have withered due to fever. Thus, it is evident that your body is still very restless and you are not fit to get up and extend hospitality to someone.

Ansooya : (to the king) Friend! You can sit on a corner of this stone platform; there is no other proper place here for you to sit.

[King sits down there. Shakuntala feels shy]

Priyambada : It is now clear that you two love each other. But I want to say something to you since you have excessive affection towards my confidante.

King : Noble lady! You express whatever is in your mind; it is not proper to keep it a secret. One has to repent later if the thought occurring in one's mind is not expressed.

Priyambada : You are the great king of this region. Hence, being the king, it is your *dharma* that you remove the troubles of your subjects.

King : But when have I opposed this idea?

Priyambada : Then, listen great king! Lord *Kaamdev* has reduced our confidante to this condition only because of you. She can survive now only if you are kind to her.

King : I am grateful to you all. In fact, even my own condition is no better.

Shakuntala : (looking towards Priyambada) Confidante! This king must be restless due to separation from queens living at his palace. Why are confusing him on this matter?

King : Beauty! My heart does not love anybody except you. You are the one with intoxicating eyes! You are the queen of my heart! If you do not believe me, I would interpret that you are again giving me wounds; and I am already injured by Cupid's arrow.

Ansooya : Great king! It is heard that kings do express love towards many queens. Therefore, make my arrangement for my confidante so that her kin do not have to regret in the future.

King : Noble lady! Athough there may be many queens in my *harem*, only two queens would be named as major in my dynasty. The first one would be Samudravasanaa, that is the earth enclosed from all directions by the oceans and the second one would be this dear confidante of yours.

Both : Then we are satisfied!

Priyambada : (looks outwards) Ansooya! Just look, this young one of a deer is looking around and searching for his mother. Come, let us take it to its mother.

[The two confidantes take steps to leave]

Shakuntala : (getting nervous) Confidantes! Who are you leaving me behind for? At least one of you ought to stay back.

Both : He, who helps the whole earth, is sitting near you. What is the cause of worry or fear then?

[Both depart]

Shakuntala : (looking towards them) Have they left?

King : Do not worry. Now, I am at your service, sitting near you. The one having beautiful thighs like an elephant's trunk! I am ready to do what pleases and gives peace to you. If you say, I can give you soothing air with the help of these cool lotus leaves which will remove your fatigue. If you say, I can put your feet in my lap. They resembles red lotus; I shall press them slowly.

Shakuntala : I do not want to earn sin by taking services of venerable persons.

[Wants to go, getting up]

King : Beauty! The day has not set yet and the condition of your body is not fine. Where would you go at this time in this scorching afternoon, leaving the floral bed and covering your bosoms with lotus leaves and with weak limbs that suffer due to separation?

[The king stops her and holds her hand]

Shakuntala : Puru king! At least maintain some dignity of modesty and virtue. I cannot do anything on my own despite the fact that I am mad in love.

King : Timid! You must stop being scared of your elders. Having profound knowledge of *dharma*, your chancellor would not be able to find any fault even if he comes to know about our affair. Many *rajarshi* maidens have married through the *Gandharva* custom. It is a fact that their fathers have only felicitated those married women.

Shakuntala : Well, kindly spare me at least now. Let me make some enquiries with my compeers.

King : I will spare you, if you say.

Shakuntala : But when?

King : As the blackbee tastefully sucks the sap of new tender flowers, thirsty like the blackbee for the juice of your lips, you will make me drink the nectar of your lips I will spare you then.

[Saying this the king wants to lift her face; Shakuntala acts as if she were weeping!]

[In the background]

Chakravak's bride! Call for your companion. Night is falling.

Shakuntala : (gets worried) Puru King! It seems that *aryaa* Gautami is coming this way to take stock of my condition. Therefore, you go behind the cover of that tree.

King : Alright.

[The king goes behind the tree. Gautami enters with an utensil in hand along with the two compeers]

Compeers : *Arye* Gautami! Come this way.

Gautami : (reaching near Shakuntala) Child! Did the fever come down?

Shakuntala : *Arye*! Indeed, it has lessened now.

Gautami : (sprinkling the water on Shakuntala's head) Fine, you will get well now with this sacred water. Child! Get up and proceed, for the day has set. Come, we return to our cottage.

[All depart]

Shakuntala : (to herself while departing) O my mind! You could not discard your timidity when your beloved was close to you to fulfill your wish. Why are you feeling upon so anguished in separation? (proceeds a few steps, then stops and speaks conspicuously) Hey, cluster of vines that removes all agonies! I extend invitation to you again.

[A gloomy Shakuntala with her compeers]

King : (returning to his originally occupied place and heaving a sigh of relief) *Aho*! There are so many obstacles, one after another, in the fulfillment of my heart's wish. The lips, which

Shakuntala had been covering time and again with her finger, could not be kissed by me. She was looking so cute even as she said 'no' repeatedly. She was turning her head towards her shoulder. I could not kiss Shakuntala who has so beautiful eyelids. Where do I go now? I can stay in that arbour in which my beloved has stayed for a while.

[After looking around]

Crushed by her body, this floral bed is lying on this rock platform. Written on the lotus leaf by her nails, this love letter is also lying here. Withered by her fever, the ornaments of lotus stem are lying here, after getting slipped from her hands. My mind is not allowing me to leave this place because so many objects are engaging my eyes.

[In the background]

O King! Demons, black like evening clouds and fearsome red, are seen roaming around the sacrificial altar as the *yajna* activities of the evening start.

King : I am coming.

[Leaves]

•

Act IV

[Both the compeers are seen acting as if they are plucking flowers]

Ansooya : Priyambada! It is a matter of great satisfaction and happiness that Shakuntala has married with *Gandharva* tradition and has found a suitable groom for herself. But I have a great worry!

Priyambada : (interrupting midway) What is the big worry?

Ansooya : The king will return to his capital after bidding adieu to us and *rishi*s, after the conclusion of *yajna* today. Then, he will be surrounded by the queens at his harem. Then, will he still remember this sacred grove?

Priyambada : It does not seem likely that he will forget all this. That is because the people, who diplay the conduct like king Dushyant, cannot be deceitful persons. But I am worried on another account.

Ansooya : What is that?

Priyambada : How would our chancellor or *maharshi* Kanva, perceive or react when he will return to the *ashram* and will come to know of her *Gandharva* marriage to the king? The subject of my worry.

Ansooya : As far as my experience suggests, he would only approve of it.

Priyambada : How can you say this?

Ansooya : Because it was his solemn resolve that he would marry her on finding a suitable groom for her. When God itself has accomplished this task, his wish has been granted without making any effort.

Priyambada : (observing the basket of flowers) Confidante! I understand that we have plucked adequate quantity of flowers for the *yajna*.

Ansooya : Yes, so much of flowers were sufficient for the *yajna*. But don't we have to worship the lord of fortune for the sake of our dear confidante Shakuntala? That worship would also require plenty of flowers.

Priyambada : Oh yes! You are right. (she begins to pluck flowers again)

[In the background]

Hey, I have already arrived.

Ansooya : (acts as if listening attentively) This seems like the voice of a guest.

Priyambada : What has happened then? Shakuntala is present at the cottage today. (thinking) But she was appearing slightly indisposed.

Ansooya : Come, let us go. The task of worship and prayer would be accomplished with these flowers.

[Both depart]

[In the background]

Hey, girl! You are the one causing disrespect to a guest. You are engrossed in whose thoughts. You are not paying heed to a hermit like me. The person you are trying to remember would forget you in spite of immense efforts of recollection in the same way as an insane person forgets his past.

[Change of scene]

Priyambada : Alas, alas! Something very unfortunate has happened. It seems as if Shakuntala, under the state of delirium due to infatuation for her husband, the king has offended a sage.

[After looking in front]

She has not offended an ordinary man. She has hurt *maharshi* Durwasa who, after invoking curse on our beloved confidante, is going back from the *ashram* at a fast pace.

Ansooya : Priyambada! You go after him, hold him back and somehow, persuade him to return. By that time, I shall fetch some water.

Priyambada : Alright. I am leaving.

[Departs]

[Ansooya moves forward a few steps and suddenly stumbles]

Ansooya : Oh my! Because of my fast pace, I have stumbled in such a way that the flower basket has slipped away from my hand.

[Ansooya picks up the flowers dropped from the basket]

[Re-entry of Priyambada]

Priyambada : Confidante! He is a very outrageous person by nature. Does he pay heed to anyone's prayer? Still, somehow I have managed to placate him a little bit.

Ansooya : (smiles) That is sufficient. Tell me, how did you console him?

Priyambada : When he did not agree to return to the *ashram* by any means, I submitted my humble request. I told *maharshi* Durwasa that it was Shakuntala's first offence. Besides, she was completely ignorant of the efficacy of the *maharshi's* brilliance. Hence, I requested that he forgive this first fault of the maiden.

Ansooya : Well, what happened after that?

Priyambada : Then he went away from there, saying that his pronouncement cannot go wrong. However, if the maiden will show to her beloved, in whose thought she was lost, an ornament or any other thing given as a souvenir by her beloved, then his curse will be revoked and her beloved will begin recognizing her.

Ansooya : Fine, at least he gave some assurance. Because the *rajarshi*, before leaving this place, had presented our confidante Shakuntala with the ring engraved with his name. He had given this to her as a memento. The very ring will prove to be an easy way for the termination of Shakuntala's curse.

Priyambada : Confidante! Come, we complete the task of God's prayer by then.

[Both turn around]

[Change of scene]

Priyambada : Ansooya! Just see, supporting her left cheek on her left hand, how our confidante appears sitting like an idol! How could she take notice of the guest when she has lost her senses by thinking about her husband?

Ansooya : Priyambada! This matter should be confined within the two of us. Shakuntala is very tender by nature; we must protect her somehow. She must not learn this matter.

Priyambada : Yes, of course. Who would be such a fool as to irrigate the vine of jasmine with hot water?

[Both depart, the curtain dropped]

[Change of scene]

[The entry of a disciple just out of bed]

Disciple : Just back from a tour, our revered *maharshi* Kanva, has asked me to observe how much of night hours are left. So, I should go outside and see how much of the night is left.

[Roams around and looks at the sky]

Oh my! It is going to be dawn. On the one hand, the moon, the master of all medicines, is departing and on the other hand, keeping its charioteer, Arun, in the front, the Sun is appearing. The rise and fall of these two luminous bodies at the same time proves that this world is regulated by its own actions. That is, happiness comes after sorrow and sorrow comes after happiness both keep on coming in a cycle.

The splendour of lotus is also waning, now that the moon has set; it does not appeal to eyes. Its glory is left to imagination only. Truly, the sorrow of separation of those women, whose husbands have gone to a foreign land, must be too agonizing to bear.

[The curtain rises]

[Entry of Ansooya]

Ansooya : Although I am ignorant about the matter of love, I understand that the king's conduct towards Shakuntala was not apt for an *Arya* to display.

[Disciple comes from the other side]

Disciple : I shall inform *guruji* that the time for *hawan* has arrived.

[Departs]

Ansooya : I have awakened. But what am I supposed to do? My hands and feet do not have strength even to carry out the daily chores today. *Kaamdev's* conscience must have been pleased after seeing that my dear confidante has invested so much faith in that liar, king Dushyanta. Or, who knows, it could be the result of Durwasa's curse that the king had not enquired after Shakuntala until now. Otherwise the *rajarshi* used to speak very sweetly. Could he not send even a letter to her beloved even after passing of so many days?

Then the ring, which he had given to Shakuntala, must be sent to him as a reminder. But I cannot comprehend who among these hermits should be sent to the capital. These people are forest dwellers; how would they know the etiquettes of the capital? How can I tell about Shakuntala's offence to revered Kanva after his returns from the trip. How would I tell him about what had happened on *rishi* Durwaasa's arrival. That Shakuntala has married king Dushyant in *Gandharva* tradition and she is pregnant too. It is almost impossible for me to utter all this. What should we do in this situation?

[Entry of Priyambada]

Priyambada : (Expressing joy) Confidante! Get up, come fast.

Ansooya : (reluctantly) Why, what is so great?

Priyambada : Confidante! Rise! The arrangements for Shakuntala's departure have to be made.

Ansooya : (expressing great surprise) How did all this happen?

Priyambada : Listen! I went to Shakuntala just a while ago. I enquired her if she slept comfortably during the night.

Ansooya : What then?

Priyambada : Revered father Kanva arrived there by then. He embraced the embarrassed Shakuntala. Giving affection, he said, "Child, today, despite being blinded by the *yajna* smoke, *yajman's* (householder who performs the sacrifice through priests) oblation fortunately dropped exactly at the same place where it should fall. Just like the mind does not repent in making an offering of education to an able disciple, I have no objection in giving you in the hands of an able spouse. I make arrangements today itself to send you along with *rishi*s to your husband's place.

Ansooya : But who told the entire detail to revered Kanva?

Priyambada : Soon, revered Kanva entered the sacrificial hall, a voice from the slay *(akashvani)* gave all the details to revered Kanva.

Ansooya : (interrupting midway out of surprise) What?

Priyambada : (attentively sings) As the fire dwells inside the tree of *Shamee*, similarly O *brahmarshi*! The ambience of Puru king Dushyant, dwells inside your daughter. Arrange to send her to her place.

Ansooya : (embracing Priyambada) Confidante! An excellent task has been accomplished. But the joy is drooping a bit due to the fact that Shakuntala will leave us today itself.

Priyambada : Confidante! We would pacify our mind somehow. But our only wish is that she should remain happy.

Ansooya : Only for such an auspicious day as today, I had retained a saffron garland having long-lasting fragrance on the coconut that is hanging from the mango branch. Do bring it down from there. By the time you fetch it, I shall arrange for such auspicious material such as *gorochan*, soil from pilgrimage sites, strands of tender grass etc.

Priyambada : Alright, you arrange all this. I shall leave now.

[Ansooya goes]

[Priyambada takes steps to bring down the garland from the mango branch]

[Change of scene]

[In the background]

Gautami, ask Sharanrav and others to get ready to accompany Shakuntala.

Priyambada : (listens attentively) Ansooya! Hurry up. The *rishi*s designated to go to Hastinapur are being called for.

[Ansooya enters with material in hand]

Ansooya : Come confidante! Let us move.

[Both depart]

[Change of scene]

Priyambada : (upon seeing Shakuntala) Watch out, Shakuntala has accomplished bathing and other chores even before daybreak. On this side, female ascetics, holding *neewar* granules in their hands, are offering blessings to her.

[Both go forward]

[Female ascetics are seen blessing Shakuntala]

First Female Ascetic: (to Shakuntala) Child! May your husband give you honour and grace you to the position of Chief Queen.

Second Female Ascetic : Child! May you become mother of a brave child.

Third Female Ascetic : Child! May you always love and adore your husband.

[All the three female ascetic depart, Gautmi stays on]

Both Compeers : (going near Shakuntala) Confidante! May today's bath of yours prove to be perpetually prosperous for you.

Shakuntala : Come compeers! You are welcome. Come and be seated.

[Both sit down keeping the auspicious utensils in their hands]

Both : Confidante! Now, sit comfortably. Now, we begin your auspicious make up.

Shakuntala : This is a matter of great fortune for me. (heaving a deep sigh) Where would I get the opportunity to be adorned by confidantes after this? (starts sobbing).

Compeers : Confidante! One does not weep on such an auspicious occasion.

[Both compeers also wipe their tears and start adorning Shakuntala]

Priyambada : Confidante! There should be very beautiful ornaments for a beauty like yours. How can the materials collected at the *ashram* adorn you?

[Two *rishi* boys enter with a present in their hands]

***Rishi* Boys** : (Offering ornaments) Take these ornaments. Adorn the goddess with this.

[All express surprise upon seeing the ornaments]

Gautami : Child Narad! Where did you get all this?

Disciple : These have been obtained through the influence of father Kanva.

Gautami : Has he produced them spontaneously through his powers acquired through religious austerity and *yajna*?

Other disciple : No! Revered Kanva had instructed us to fetch flowers and leaves from the vines and trees for the ornamentation of Shakuntala. Some trees offered auspicious clothes, some offered *mahaavar* (red colour used by ladies to beautify their feet) *Vandevis*, competing with the buds, gave away many ornaments.

Priyambada : (seeing Shakuntala) Confidante! These precursors reveal that you would become *Rajlakshmi* at your husband's home and enjoy all the luxuries of life.

[Shakuntala acts shy]

First Disciple: Gautam, come let us move. Our chancellor has arrived after taking bath. Let us thank the vegetation for granting so much to us for Shakuntala.

Second Disciple : Yes, move.

[Both depart]

Compeers : Confidante! We have never seen ornaments, leave alone wearing them. But we adorn your body with them just like we have seen in paintings.

Shakuntala : I am well aware of your skill. You never do anything wrong.

[Compeers dress up Shakuntala with the ornaments]

[Change of scene]

[Entry of Kanva rishi; he has returned after taking a bath]

Kanva : Shakuntala will leave today; my heart is sinking due to this grief. My throat has choked and my mouth cannot emanate words. When a forest dweller like me is so much agonized, what would happen to those poor who send off their daughters for the first time.

[Roams about in desperation]

Compeers : Shakuntala! We have completed your decoration. Now, you wear this silken pair of clothes yourself.

[Shakuntala gets up, starts dressing up]

Gautami : Child! Revered Kanva is coming this way. His eyes are brimming with the tears of joy. If one looks at his eyes, one imagines as if he is embracing you with his eyes itself. Do pay respect to him.

Shakuntala : (feeling shy) Revered father! My respect.

Kanva : Child! May your husband pay respect to you as Yayati had honoured his wife, Sharmishtha. May you have a son, monarch of the world, like Sharmishtha's son Puru.

Gautmi : Lord! You have given a boon to Shakuntala, not a blessing.

Kanva : Child! Proceed now. Take a round around the holy *yajna* fire which has received some *ahuti* a short while ago.

[All circle around]

Kanva : (offers blessing by chanting the *Rigveda's* verse)

Amee vedi paritah kliraptdhisnya-
samidhwantahprantsansteernadarbhaah,
Apdhyanatanduritam havyagandhairvaitanastwam vahnayah pavyantu.

Now proceed.

[Looks around]

Where are Sharanrav and others?

Disciple : (enters) Lord! We are ready and waiting.

Kanva : Go and accompany your sister.

Sharanrav : Come this way O goddess.

[All walk]

Kanva : O the trees of the *tapovan* that is replete with forest gods! She never used to drink water without watering you. She never touched your delicate leaves, despite the fact that she loves ornaments. She was always delighted upon seeing your new buds. The same Shakuntala is going home. You see her off her love.

[Cooing of a cuckoo is heard]

Kanva : (pointing towards the cuckoo) The trees, who were Shakuntala's companions of the forest, and other birds have the cuckoo's voice for her to set out for house.

[From the sky]

May the journey of Shakuntala be fruitful. Ponds teeming with blue lotus on her way! May there be trees planted intermittently with dense shadow to save her from sunshine. May the dust have the delicacy of the lotus pollen and may the breeze, offering succour, keep blowing on the way to her home.

[All listen with surprise]

Gautami : Child! The *vandevi*s, who have been dear to you like kin, are offering their blessings to you. Do pay respect to them.

Shakuntala : (bows and salutes *vandevis*, then turns and takes Priyambada aside) Compeer Priyambada! Although I am excessively eager to visit *Aryaputra* at this time, yet my feet are not moving forward. I do not want to leave the *ashram*.

Priyambada : It is not only you who is grief-stricken due to the separation from the sacred grove. As the time of your departure is coming near, the sacred grove also appears to be sad.

Have a look. The deer are regurgitating the chewed morsels of the grass. Peacocks have stopped dancing. The yellow leaves are falling from the vines in such a way as if they were their tears!

Shakuntala : (recalling) Father! I am going to meet my sister-like vine, *Van-jyotsana*.

Kanva : Yes, I know that you give affection to her like your true sister. Look, she is there, towards the right. Go, and greet her.

Shakuntala : (Going near the vine and clinging to it) Dear *Van-jyotsana!* In spite of being clung to the mango tree, do embrace me in the arms of your branches. I am going far away from you.

Kanva : By the influence of your sacred acts, you have found the kind of husband I had resolved to arrange for you. *Van-jyotsana* has also got the suitable shelter in the form of this mango tree. Now I am free from the worry of you two. Come and move through this way.

Shakuntala : (to compeers) Compeers! I am leaving this *Van-jyotsana* to your care.

Compeers : And in whose care are you leaving us?

[All compeers start crying]

Kanva : Do not cry Ansooya! On the contrary, you are supposed to console Shakuntala.

[All turn around]

Shakuntala : Father! When this doe, moving leisurely around the *ashram* due to the burden of embryo, deliver a young one comfortably, arrange to send this happy news to me through somebody. Please do not forget.

Kanva : Not at all! We shall certainly communicate the news to you.

[All act to move ahead]

Shakuntala : (acts as if there is an obstruction in her movement) Hey! Who is pulling back the border of my *sari*?

[Turns back to see]

Kanva : Child! You used to apply Higota oil after it hurt its mouth by eating *kusha* (grass). You used to feed him a fistful of millet grains everyday. The same affectionate deer is stopping you from leaving the *ashram*.

Shakuntala : Hey! I am going, leaving the company of you all. Why are you following me please go back? I had brought you up when your mother had died after giving birth to you. Now, father will take care of you in my absence.

[Moves ahead sobbing]

Kanva : Child! Wipe your tears; have patience. These beautiful eyes of yours are not able to see clearly due to these tears. Therefore, you are putting your steps improperly on the rough and rugged land of this place. Lest your foot should receive a sprain.

Sharanrav : Lord! It is heard that those, who come to see off some dear one, should return after accompanying up to a water pond. The bank of the pond is visible. So, all of you should return to the *ashram* from this point. If you have any message for the great king, Dushyant, please tell me now.

Kanva : Well then, let us sit for a while under the shadow of this *peepul* tree.

[All sit down]

Kanva : (talks to himself) What message should be sent?

[Acts as if thinking]

Shakuntala : (separately to the confidante) Confidante! Just watch, how this ruddy-goose is screaming due to worry it is not being able to locate its gander which is hidden in the cover of lotus leaves. This is the sign of ill-omen. Therefore, I do not foresee that the task for which I am going is likely to be accomplished.

Ansooya : Confidante! You should not think in this manner. This ruddy-goose too spends the long nights of separation, for it is far away from her husband; it feels lonely too. Nevertheless, it maintains hope during this separation that it will certainly unite with its beloved in the morning.

Kanva : Sharanrav! While handing Shakuntala over to Dushyant, tell him on my behalf that.

Sharanrav : (interrupts) Yes sir, give me command.

Kanva : Tell him thus. King! We are the simple disciplined hermits who dwell in the forest and you are the inheritor of a great lineage, for you are the king's son. There is no comparison between you and us. Still, you yourself have married this maiden. Keeping these things in mind, you are expected to confer respect on Shakuntala which must be akin to that conferred on the other queens.

If she receives greater fortune than this, it would be a matter of her luck. What we, the kin of this maiden, can say to you about that?

Sharanrav : Father! I have understood your intention.

Kanva : (beckons Shakuntala and calls her near him) Child! Come, I have to teach you something. Despite the fact that we live in the forest, we are fully aware of the worldly etiquettes and customs.

Sharanrav : What are the issues that learned people do not know?

Kanva : Child! When you arrive at your husband's home offer good service and care to all the elders of the house. Have affection for other wives and treat them as compeers. Do not fight even if your husband treats you disrespectfully. Confer great affection on attendants, male or female, and never boast of your good fortune.

Only those women, who maintain such type of conduct in their house, happen to be good housewives. And those, who act opposite to it, are called flawed women. Am I right Gautami?

Gautami : What would be a better lesson for a bride of good family than this? Child! Make a note of these things.

Kanva : Child! Come, do embrace me and your compeers.

Shakuntala : Father! Will Priyambada, Ansooya and other compeers return from here only?

Kanva : Child! I have to get them marry as well. It is not suitable for them to go along with you to the royal palace. Gautami will go along with you.

Shakuntala : (embracing father) How would I be able to spend my life away from the lap of father. I would be like the uprooted trees of the mountain Malaya, literally!

Kanva : Child! Why are you being so impatient? After, becoming the chief queen of a king of very high lineage, you will remain busy in his household tasks night and day. Just like the direction of east leads to the emergence of the sun, you will also give birth to a holy son. Then you yourself will forget the sorrow of separation from us.

[Shakuntala falls on the feet of her father]

Kanva : (offering blessing) May you get all that I have wished for you.

Shakuntala : (going to compeers) Compeers! You all come together and embrace me.

Compeers : (in the state of embrace) Confidante! See, if the king makes a mistake in recognizing you, show him the ring bearing his name that you have with you.

Shakuntala : Why are you saying so? Your statement has apprehension in my mind.

Compeers : No, do not be afraid. Such things do happen in love.

Sharanrav : *Devi*! The day has advanced and it would be afternoon pretty soon. Now make haste.

Shakuntala : (facing towards *ashram*) Father! When would I be able to visit the *ashram* again?

Kanva : When you will live for long as his wife on this earth and when providing king Dushyant with a brave and extraordinary son like him. Later, leaving the responsibility of the kingdom and the family on him, you and your husband will set out from the royal palace. Then, you would come to this quiet *ashram* to live peacefully.

Gautami : Child! The time of departure is ticking away. Now, let father go back. (to *maharshi* Kanva)

Now you should go back, otherwise she will keep asking one question or the other.

Kanva : Child! Now, I have to go for my austerity; it is getting late for that.

Shakuntala : (meeting with father once again) You have become very feeble due to meditation. Therefore, do not worry about me in any case.

Kanva : (heaving a sigh) child! My grief will not lessen until the sprouts of the seeds, which you had sown for sacrifice at the door of the cottage, will be visible. Proceed, now. May your journey be auspicious!

[Departure of Shakuntala along with companions]

Both Compeers : (watching Shakuntala) Ah! Shakuntala has gone out of sight behind the cover of trees.

Kanva : (taking a deep sigh) Ansooya! Your confidante has gone now. Stop lamenting and return to *ashram* along with me.

Both compeers : Father! How will we fill up this vacuum in the absence of Shakuntala?

Kanva : These things do happen. (contemplating and taking a round) Oh! I am feeling better after sending Shakuntala to her husband's home.

A daughter truly belongs to another. I have accomplished my task after sending her. That way, my mind has become free from worry.

[Thus all leave]

[The curtain drops]

•

Act V

[King is seated on a seat and the Jester is also sitting along with him]

Jester : (listens attentively) Friend! Listen, pay heed to the music room. Someone is singing a sweet song in quite a mellifluous voice in a fine rhythm and tune. It seems as queen Hanspadika is practicing music.

King : If you keep quiet, then only can I listen.

[Song in the background]

Greedy of honey, o blackbee,
In the gluttony of new honey,
Just in one attempt,
Sweet cluster of blossoms juicy,
You have kissed all,
Dweller of lotus shell,
O blackbee,
Why did you,
Forget me.

King : Perfect! A fine love stream seems to be flowing in this note as well.

Jester : But have you tried to understand the sarcasm implicit in this song?

King : (smiling) Yes! I have understood. I have made amorous supplication with the queen only once. Nowadays, I have started loving *devi* Vasumatee. This song is being sung in that background. Confidant Madhavya! You go to Hanspadika and tell her on my behalf that she has made a nice, sweet sarcastic remark. Tell her that she is quite skilled in the art and science of reproach.

Jester : (getting up) As your command. But friend! Just as great persons renowned for detachment and *rishi*s are not able to stop themselves falling in the hands of celestial damsels, she will catch me from my lock of hair. Then, attendants would start beating me, I would find my release quite difficult then.

King : Go, use a bit of adroitness in delivering the message.

Jester : There is no other way; I have to go.

[Jester leaves]

King : (internally) Why is my mind feeling indisposed while listening to this song, in spite of the fact that all my close kinfolks are here with me? When even *muj nin* too becomes indisposed upon seeing beautiful things and listening to sweet words, it should be understood that the traditions and values of the beloveds from the previous birth might have revived automatically.

[King becomes agonized upon thinking this]

[Change of scene]

[The chamberlain enters into the king's chamber the very moment]

Chamberlain : Ah, where have I reached now?

The stick, which, at one point of time, used to be in my hand as for the symbol of doorkeeper of the queen's apartment, has become a support for my staggering feet at this old age. It is understandable that the great king should perform religious deeds. He has just gone from here, the seat of justice. But these disciples of Kanva have made a sudden appearance. I do not feel like communicating about their arrival. But I am helpless; There is no rest for a royal servant! Where is leisure even for the king? Having yoked his chariot once, even the Sun is constantly on the move, till now. *Sheshnaag* too has been inexorably holding the load of the earth since day one. The same is the condition with the king who accepts one sixth part of the crop as royal tax. Therefore, I should also proceed and execute my duty.

[Seeing here and there]

Well, the great king is sitting. Having become tired after accomplishing the tasks of his subjects, the great king is relaxing here in solitude in the same way in which a big tusker, scorched due to the sunshine and leaving the herd of elephants to graze, takes rest at a cool place.

[Going near the king]

Victory to the great king! A few hermits, the inhabitants of the Himalayan valley, have arrived with the message of *maharshi* Kanva. They are accompanying two women also. Now, command as you deem fit.

King : Have some hermits arrived with the message of *maharshi* Kanva?

Chamberlain: Yes sir.

King : Then ask family priest, Somraatji, on my behalf to accord suitable welcome with Vedic tradition to these *ashram* dwellers and bring them to me. By that time, I also go to take a seat at a place where it would be proper to meet with the *rishi*s.

Chamberlain: As per your wish, O great king.

[Departs]

King : (after getting up) Vetravati! Please take me to the *yajna* hall.

Doorkeeper : Great king! Come, this way.

King : (roams about, and then narrates about the difficulties in discharging the royal duties) All other living beings enjoy upon securing everything they wish. But when the wish of becoming the king is fulfilled for persons like us, we observe that it is only the troubles that have been gained.

One feels great to become a king but the difficulties faced during the execution of state affairs pushes one into an adverse situation.

[Change of scene]

[In the background]

Two minstrels: Victory to the great king!

First Minstrel: You engage relentlessly in the welfare of public, casting aside the desire of your own comfort. Or, you are complying with your *dharma* by doing so. You are like a tree endures harsh heat of the sun on its head but provides only shadow to every creature that sits under it.

Second Minstrel: You control with your royal scepter, those people who go on the wrong path or are evil. You settle the disputes that arise between warring factions. In this way, you are always prepared to protect your subjects. Those, who have good amount of wealth, have many kith and kin. Alternatively, many people go close to them. But you are the final authority for the common man. Who else do they have in this world to relay on except you?

King : (after listening) Even my distressed mind has become delighted after listening to your sweet talk.

[Moves about]

Doorkeeper : (to the king) Great king! The sitting room of the *yajna* hall is this way. Have a look, it has been made spic and span after dusting and cleaning. Nearby has been fastened the cow whose milk is used for *hawan*. Come great king! Please have your seat.

King : (stands up with the help of attendants after ascending) Vetravati! What could be the purpose behind lord Kanva sending his *rishi*s to me? Did the miscreant demons again start creating trouble for these *rishi*s who observe severe austerity? Or did anybody else harass these inhabitants of the sacred grove who practise *dharma*? Or, did the blooming of vines and trees stop due to my sins? I don't know, how many such doubts have begun to arise in my mind. Since I am not able to guess properly, my mind is getting very fretful.

Doorkeeper : Great king! Why do you think so? My mind says that pleased with the king's acts of religious duties, these *rishi*s must have come to congratulate you.

[Entry of chamberlain and priest followed by Gautami and *rishi*s; they keep Shakuntala at the front]

Chamberlain : (showing them the passageway) Come, this way you O sages and respected guests.

Sharanrav : Shardwat! I am sure that this king is such a virtuous man that he has never violated his propriety of conduct. Even the people of lower rank in his kingdom do not engage themselves in illegitimate deeds. Nevertheless, my solitude-loving mind is still suggesting that I should escape from here somehow. Why is it happening?

Shardwat : Because you normally live in the sacred grove. It is quite natural after coming to the city. I also look down upon these people who are steeped in the worldly pleasures.

Shakuntala : (pointing towards a bad omen) Why is my right eye fluttering?

Gautami : (extending assurance) Daughter! May your bad omens go away. May your husband and the family deity confer blessing on you.

[Turns]

Priest : (signaling towards the king) Austere gentlemen! Look, the great king who practices *varnashram dharma*, is waiting anxiously for your arrival. He has already stood up from his seat to welcome you.

Sharanrav : Sir, we are aware of the fact that this great king is worthy of praise. But that is not important for us.

Trees do bend upon bearing fruit. Saturated with water, new clouds do hang low; similarly, those, who are noble, become humble, not haughty, upon obtaining wealth and honour.

Doorkeeper : (to the king) Great king! *Rishi*s appear cheerful. It can be guessed that these people have arrived here for some purpose.

King : (seeing towards Shakuntala) Who could be this lady?

Who could this be amidst these hermits, appearing like a new sapling among the yellow leaves? Her beauty is not showing properly due to her veil. Nevertheless, she is somewhat different from the hermits.

Doorkeeper : Great king! I am curious and I also want to know the same. But I am unable to understand. It can be guessed from whatever is visible that she is very beautiful.

King : You could be right. But throwing a glance towards someone else's woman is not an appropriate act.

Shakuntala : (thinking while, placing hand on her heart) O heart! Why are you beating so fast? Have some patience, keeping the love of *Aryaputra* in mind.

Priest : (coming forward) Great king! I have methodically performed worship of these hermits. Their hospitality rituals have been accomplished. Their great guru has sent a message through them. That is meant for you; hence you only can listen to it.

King : I am grateful.

***Rishi*s** : (raising their hands) Victory to great king.

King : I greet you all.

***Rishi*s** : May your wish has be fulfilled.

King : Are the sages facing any problem while carrying out *yajna* or meditation?

***Rishi*s** : There is no such problem sir. Can anyone cause obstruction in the religious chores of the grove when a brilliant king like you is ready to protect the earth?

King : Hence, my kingship has become meaningful to my subjects.

Is *maharshi* Kanva, engaged in the welfare of the world, feeling fine?

Rishis : O Great king! After asking about your well being, he has sent a message for....

King : (interrupts) Yes, yes! What command has he sent?

Sharanrav : He has asked us to say that he has become happy knowing about the marriage that you had solemnized with his daughter under *Gandharva* tradition. You are understood to be the foremost among honourable persons. Shakuntala is the perfect embodiment of holy acts.

So, you should accept this pregnant woman by making her your wife.

Gautami : *Arya*! I also want to say something. Although I should not speak amidst you. I speak for Shakuntala's welfare. Neither Shakuntala discussed with her elders nor you enquired anything from her kith and kin. When you two decided everything mutually and in solitude, what can I say to you?

Shakuntala : (thinking) Let us watch what does *aryaputra* say now.

King : What are you people saying?

Shakuntala : (internally) When he speaks, it seems as if he were emitting fire!

Sharanrav : Why are you talking like this when you are aware of all the etiquettes of social norms? People pass unsavory comments about the woman who, howsoever chaste, lives at her father's house while her husband is alive. Therefore, the near and dear ones of this young woman, want her to live with her husband.

King : Did I get married at some earlier occasion to this *devi*?

Shakuntala : (thinking and filled with sorrow) O my heart! What you had feared is now appearing before you.

Sharanrav : Are you repentant about your deed, or are you turning away from your duty. Alternatively, do you want to forget your acts deliberately?

King : I am unable to understand what you are saying. How did this false imagination come to your mind?

Sharanrav : Such thoughts are generally found in those who are intoxicated due to affluence.

Gautami : (to Shakuntala) Child! Leave the shame and decency for the time being. Come, I shall raise your veil. At least your husband should be able to recognize you that way.

[Raises Shakuntala's veil]

King : (thinking upon seeing Shakuntala carefully) I am not able to understand properly if ever had married this beautiful woman. Therefore, my situation at this moment has become similar to that of a blackbee which can neither sit on the *kund* flower (a kind of jasmine) covered with dew in the morning nor can go elsewhere leaving. I am unable to neither accept nor desert her (keeps contemplating like that).

Doorkeeper : (thinking) Our great king is a noble person. Otherwise, who would think about the welfare of such a beautiful maiden who has come to him all by herself?

Sharanrav : Why have you turned silent?

King : Hermits! I have tried to recall repeatedly but cannot recall any thing. I have ever married this *devi* is not striking my memory. In that condition, advice me how, by accepting this *devi* with obvious signs of pregnancy, can I invite the infamy of being the husband of a woman who is pregnant due to some other man?

Shakuntala : (thinking) *Aryaputra* is now doubtful about the occurrence of marriage. In that case, it is futile to even think of the great expectations that I had fostered for him.

Sharanrav : Alright, you do not accept her. You are insulting a *rishi* who, being generous, was considering you a deserving candidate. He was offering you her daughter. You have spoiled her by deceit.

Shardwat : Sharanrav! You keep quiet for some time, to Shakuntala. Shakuntala! We have already said whatever we had to say or whatever we could have said. But we see no effect of it on the king. Therefore, it is upon you to make him believe our story.

Shakuntala : (thinking) When the king is not prepared to recall anything, what would be the use of reminding him of the love that he had expressed at that time? Now my misfortune alone has remained in my life.

((Overtly) *Aryaputra*! (stops speaking, thinking) This type of address to him is not proper now when he has doubts about our marriage. (addresses again) *Pururaj!* It does not behave of you to behave with me sans respect, given that you were the one who had lured me into the nupital relationship through your sweet talk.

King : (covering his ears) *Shaant paapam.*

What are you saying? Why do you want to bring disrepute to your clan and also push me towards destruction?

Shakuntala : Well, if you truly consider me an unfamiliar woman, I show you a memento to remove your doubt.

King : Yes, show me.

Shakuntala : (gropes her finger) Alas! Misfortune. Where did the ring go from my finger?

(Looks helplessly towards Gautami)

Gautami : (after thinking) When you were paying obeisance to the waters of *Shacheeteerthha* during *Shakravatar*, the ring might have slipped from your finger and fallen into the waters.

King : (smiling) Someone has rightly stated that women have swift intelligence.

Shakuntala : My misfortune did not spare me here too. Well, I shall try to give you another proof.

King : The time for showing is over; it is time for narrating.

Shakuntala : You might remember that one day, you were standing with water in a cup of lotus leave at the jasmine arbour of our *ashram*.

King : Yes, go on. I am listening.

Shakuntala : At that very moment, a baby deer named Deerghapang, which I had nursed like my son, arrived there. You had said out of compassion, "Let it drink water first."

Saying this you started giving it water to drink. Since it was unfamiliar to you, it did not come near you. Then I took the leaf cup from your hands and offered it water. It began drinking water. At that time, you had said amusingly that one recognizes one's kith and kin and so jokingly asked whether both of us were forestdwellers. Can't you recall that incident?"

King : Only licentious people fall into the trap of such false and sweet talks of women like you.

Gautami : *Mahabhag*! It is not proper for you to talk like this! This girl, grown up in the sacred grove, is completely ignorant of fraud and deceit.

King : Respected old hermit! Even females that are not human species become very clever without training and education; then, what can one state about the intelligent women of this type? Don't you know that the cuckoo, whose voice seems sweet to everybody, displays such cleverness that she keeps its young ones at the nests of the other birds and makes its young ones until they are ready to fly. At least, you should know all this.

Shakuntala : (angrily) *Anarya* (not noble)! You want to prove all others as wily and corrupt, thinking that they are just like you. Who would be so mean other than you, to do such abominable deed under the guise of *dharma.*

King : (thinking) Doubt is taking over my mind upon seeing her anger. Therefore, my mind is sinking further into an abyss of uncertainty. That is because Shakuntala, who has raised her eyebrows and has eyes red due to anger, is agitated due to such a harsh refusal of the love committed in solitude. True, I cannot recall properly and my denial has broken *Kaamdev's* (Cupid's) bow into two pieces.

[Openly]

Bhadrey (noble lady)! The entire world is aware of Dushyant's deeds. But such a heinous talk has not been heard till date.

Shakuntala : Probably, you have done the right thing by making me a characterless woman. Because of my false impression about your great family, I have fallen in hands. You are a mean man who has honey in his mouth but whose heart is full of venom.

[Covering her face with the border of her sari, she starts crying]

Sharanrav : This kind of sorrow is accorded to the people for the deeds which they don't do thoughtfully. Secret love should be given and taken after great forethought. That is because friendship made with a person whose nature is not known changes into enmity one day.

King : Sir! Why are you blaming me with such words and why are you believing this lady?

Sharanrav : (angrily, he is calling to his companions) Did you all listen to his irrational talks? Treat her a liar who has not heard even the name of deceit since birth. Here's the king, devoted to truth but has learnt the trick to deceive due to his education.

King : Well mister truthful! I presume that I am just the one you are describing. But tell me what would I gain by tricking this lady?

Sharanrav : Degeneration, downfall!

King : Who can accept that the family of Puru will have downfall?

Shardwat : Sharanrav! What is the use of such a debate? We have delivered the message of revered *guruji* to him. Hence, we must go back now.

[Pointing towards the king]

King! She is your wife. You keep her with honour or oust her from home. That is because a husband has full rights over his wife.

Gautami : You lead us.

[They take steps to depart]

Shakuntala : This conman has only cheated me and now, you too are going, leaving me here?

[She also starts walking behind them]

Gautami : (stops) Child Sharanrav! See Shakuntala, all in tears, is coming after us. Now, tell me what should my daughter do being turned down by such an unkind man?

Sharanrav : (returns angrily towards her) You wily woman! Why do you want to act so arbitrarily?

[Shakuntala shakes due to fear]

Sharanrav : Shakuntala! Listen to me.

If what the king is saying is true, a fallen women like you have no role to play at her father's home, for you are deemed a blot on the entire clan. But you must live even as a maidservant at your husband's home, if you consider yourself pure and justified. You stay here. We are leaving.

King : Venerated sage! Why are you keeping this poor fellow in the dark? That is because as, the moon helps bloom only lilies and the sun bloom only lotuses, similarly persons in full control of their senses do not wish even to touch others' women.

Sharanrav : Why should you fear harem *adharma* if you can forget the events of the past after visiting your harem queens?

King : (asks his priest) I request you to tell me about right and wrong in this situation. Either I have forgotten or she is telling a lie. In this situation, should I commit the sin of deserting my wife or touching a woman who belongs to someone?

Priest : (after some contemplation) If that is so, then you do one thing.

King : Sir, please order.

Priest : Let this *devi* live at my house until she gives birth to the child. You might like to know why I am saying so. The reason is that *rishi*s and *muni*s have blessed you already that you would have a son. They have also stated that he would be the sovereign of the world. If the son of Shakuntala, the grandson of Kanva *rishi*, will show all the signs of the sovereign of the world, you can respectfully give her a place in your queen's apartment. If those signs are not found in the child, you can send her back to her father.

King : *Guruji!* Do as you deem fit.

Priest : (to Shakuntala) Daughter! Come, along with me.

Shakuntala : O mother Earth! You blast open so that I could disappear into you.

[Thus crying, Shakuntala follows the priest and *rishi*s. Devoid of memory due to the curse, the king broods over Shakuntala]

[Change of scene]

[In the background]

It is amazing; it is startling. What is it that happened?

King : (listens attentively) What has happened now?

[Priest enters]

Priest : (astounded) Great king! An amazing incidence has taken place.

King : Why, what has happened?

Priest : Great king! After the departure of the disciples of Kanva *rishi*, the *rishi* daughter started weeping by opening her arms. Then ...

King : (curiously) What happened them?

Priest : At that very moment, feminine flame appeared there, the *rishi* daughter in her lap went towards *apsara* pilgrimage.

[All express astonishment]

King : Lord! I had already deserted her. You had devised a way and tried to take her to your house. However, she went elsewhere. Therefore, it is useless to think about her now. Please go home and relax.

Priest : Victory to the great king.

[Departure of the priest]

King : (to the doorkeeper) Vetravati! My conscience has begun to be greatly distressed. I want to relax.

Doorkeeper : Great king! Come this way.

[Leads the way]

King : (thinking) I have insulted and rejected her to the hilt because of my lack of awareness about the marriage. However, my heart tends to believe her story time and again. I don't know why a heart ache has been bothering me for quite some time.

[All depart]

[Curtain drops]

•

Act VI

[Entrance of King's brother-in-law, a city guard and a chained person, surrounded by two guards]

Both Guards : (thrashing the prisoner) Speak thief! How did this gem-studded ring, engraved with our king's name, come to you? Speak up now!

Prisoner : (petrified) Have mercy *maharaj*! I have never committed theft.

First Guard : So, did the great king donate this ring to you, considering that you were a deserving Brahmin?

Prisoner : No *maharaj*! It is not so. Please do listen to me. I am a fisherman, living near Shakravatar village.

Second Guard: Hey thief! Are we asking about your caste?

King's brother-in-law : *Soochak!* You are not allowing him to speak. Let him express himself properly; do not interrupt in between.

Guard : As your command! Alright speak up now, what were you saying?

Prisoner : With my net, hook, and rod, I catch fish from the river. I earn my livelihood through this and bred my family this way...

Shyamal : You have a great undertaking at hand.

The person : Please do not say that, *maharaj!* O master! God has given this task to our caste, be it good or bad. Now, we cannot do away with this profession. Now see and understand. Although killing animals is a sin, it is heard that great compassionate and well-read brahmins also sacrifice animals during the course of *yajna*.

Shyamal : Well, stop preaching and speak up.

The person : I caught a *rohu* fish one day. When I was cutting it, I saw this shining, gem-studded ring inside it. As I was displaying it in the market to sell it, I was arrested by your guards. This is the story of the procurement of this ring. Now, the decision is yours whether you punish me or set me free.

Shayamal : Januk! It is beyond doubt that he is a fish-eating fisherman because his body stinks of raw flesh and fish. In so far, as the ring is concerned, he has stated that he had turned it from the stomach of a fish. We should go and verify it. It would be appropriate to produce him before the great king first.

Guards : Okay, You proceed, fisherman!

[Both guards take away the fisherman]

[Change of scene]

Shyamal : *Soochak!* I am going to the great king to deliver the news of the recovery of his ring. Until, I give the news to him and I return with his orders, you protect this man. You stay here at the city gate.

Both : Yes, you go. Master, you proceed towards the palace.

[Shyamal walks off]

[The guards wait for long]

First Guard : *Januk!* He is quite late, for he has not returned yet.

Second Guard: Brother! One can meet the king only after getting an opportunity; and one can talk to him according to the appropriateness of situation.

First Guard : Januk! I am feeling a pleasant itching in my palms. I am foreseeing a garland of red flowers that we are likely to wear as the reward of executing this man.

[Saying this, points towards the fisherman]

The Person : Brother! Why are you anxious to kill me? I have not committed any crime.

Second Guard : (seeing some one coming from a distance) Look, our master is coming this way holding the king's order in his hand.

Your time is over. Now, you would either become food for vultures or be eaten up by dogs.

[Entry of Shyamal]

Shyamal : *Soochak!* Set this fisherman free.

Guard : Why master?

Shyamal : His description of the ring is correct.

Soochak : As per your command, master.

Januk : Hey, You have returned from the door of *Yamraj* (the god of death).

[The chain of the prisoner is removed]

Prisoner : (paying obeisance to Shyamal) Tell me master! How did you get the testimony of my statement?

Shyamal : Take it, the great king has offered to you the money equivalent to the price of the ring as a token of gratification.

[Hands over the small bundle of money to the fisherman]

Fisherman : (receives the money and pays obeisance to Shyamal) Master! I thank you for this kindness.

Soochak : True! This is what I call kindness. What else could it be? A man has been put on the top of an elephant after being removed from gallows.

Januk : (says to Shyamal) Master! You have termed it gratification but it is reward and not gratification. Hence, we should call it reward. It seems that the great king has liked the ring.

Shyamal : It is not so, *Jaanuk!* The great king did not take that ring due to its studded jewels; rather, he was reminded of someone very dear to him after seeing the ring. Although our king is very sober by nature, he had become quite indisposed for some time after seeing the ring.

Soochak : Master! Then, you have indeed accomplished a great task for our great king.

Januk : You can also say that a fisherman has done a great job for the king.

[Looks toward the fisherman with envy]

Fisherman : (to Shyamal) Master! I offer half of this reward to you as present.

Januk : Yes, he is right.

Shyamal : *Dheevar!* You have become very dear friend of mine from today. Let us strengthen our friendship with a couple a pegs of liquor. Let us go to drinking house.

[All depart]

[Change of scene]

[Riding an aircraft in the sky, the celestial damsel, Sanumati enters]

Sanumati : Today, it was my turn to look after *Apsara* pilgrim during the bathing course of saints. I have finished that job. Now, I proceed and check the condition of *rajarshi*. Although Shakuntala is the daughter of Menaka. Now, she is my daughter too due to this relation. Long ago, Menaka had asked me to find a solution for her daughter.

[Looking around]

Aha! spring festival is round the corner. However, close but the royal house is completely engulfed in silence. Although I can see and judge everything through my divine eyes, I must honour the words of my confidante. Well, I hide myself with the help of the art of *tiraskarini*. Thus, moving along with these female gardeners, I shall try to get the news about this place.

[Descends from the aircraft and stands at the ground]

[One female attendant enters and watches the blossoming mango tree, another female attendant comes close to her]

First Attendant : O the life and soul of the spring season! The auspicious form of spring! Hey blossoms of red, green and yellow coloures! It is the first glimpse of you all in this season. Kindly be pleased with us so that this spring season passes comfortably for us.

Second Attendant : Hey cuckoo! Why are you chirping all alone?

First Attendant : The cuckoo is bound to get intoxicated upon seeing the mango bloom.

Second Attendant : (goes to her with great merriment and says) Confidante! Has the spring come?

First attendent: (pointing towards female blackbee) O female blackbee! These are your days for humming with joy.

Second Attendant : Confidante! If you help me, I would collect these mango blooms for today's prayer.

First Attendant: I am ready to assist you if you offer one half of the reward of your worship to me.

Second Attendant: Hey! You would have got that without your askance. That is because we are two bodies and one soul.

[The first attendant assists and the second one plucks mango blooms]

Wow! Although these mango blooms have not blossomed fully, their fragrance is delightful beyond compare.

[With her palms joined together]

O! Cluster of mango blossoms! I offer you to lord *Kaamdev* (Cupid). May you become the sharpest of the five arrows of *Kaamdev* so that you may give lustful passion to the youthful women whose men have gone to foreign lands.

[Saying this, she drops the cluster of mango blossoms downwards]

[Change of scene]

[The chamberlain enters by yanking at the curtain]

Chamberlain : (in an angry tone) No! Imprudent lasses. What are you doing? Why are you plucking mango blooms when you know that the great king has ordered to halt the spring festival?

Both : (frightened) Sir, do not be angry; we did not have knowledge of this fact.

Chamberlain : Did you people not hear?

Both : What is it, *arye*?

Chamberlain : Even trees that blossom during spring season and the birds that chirp on them have obeyed the command of the great king, leave alone the common man look!

The cluster of blossoms had arrived early on the mango fruits but they are still devoid of pollen. The flower of *kurbak* wanted to bloom but did not; It is still knotted as such. The winter has passed but cuckoo's voice has not been heard yet. As if it has stuck having come up to her throat. Kaamdev also pulls out arrow from his quiver but puts it back out of fear. He no longer shoots with his arrows.

Sanumati : There is no doubt about it. This means *rajarshi* is a very glorious king.

First Attendant : Sir, Mitravasu, the guard of this city, had appointed us in the service of the great king to watch this Pramad forest only a few days ago. We are totally new to this place. Hence, we had no knowledge of this thing. Had we known it we would have never plucked the blossoms.

Chamberlain : Never mind. Now do not do any such thing again.

Both : Sir! we are very curious to know why the great king has decided not to celebrate the spring festival. Kindly tell us, if you do not have any reluctance in informing why the great king stop the spring festival.

Sanumati : Man loves to celebrate and enjoy festivals. There must be a sound reason behind it if the great king has stopped the festival. Otherwise, it was not easy to stop a celebration like the spring festival.

Chamberlain : No, there is no hitch in telling you because this matter is known to all. Therefore, I shall tell you too. Have you heard the story of desertion of Shakuntala by the king?

Both : Yes sir. The news of the receipt of the ring by the great king is known to us. The city guard told us the entire story.

Chamberlain : So, there is little for you people to know. Upon the ring the great king, suddenly recalled that he had married Shakuntala under the *Gandharva* tradition. He realized that he had deserted her due to a mistake. Since then, he has been excessively remorseful.

Beautiful things do not appeal to him. He does not preside over court meetings. Even during the night, sleep evades him. He keeps tossing in the bed during the entire night.

When the queens from queen's apartment want to know the cause of this condition, nothing comes through his mouth. Shakuntala's name is uttered in a fit, though.

After that, he keeps his head low for long time due to shame.

Sanumati : This is an interesting news for me.

Chamberlain : That is why he has stopped the spring festival due to this anguish.

Both : Yes, he has done a right thing. How can he celebrate if his mind has no joy?

[In the background]

Come great king!

Chamberlain : (listens attentively) Hey! The great king is coming this way. Now, you go and carry on with your job.

Both : Alright.

[Both depart]

[Entry of remorseful king along with the jester and doorkeeper]

Chamberlain : (upon the king) Those, who have good looks appear good-looking, irrespective of their condition, that is, in all conditions. Our great king is looking good despite being sad. He has taken off all the ornaments that used to decorate his body; only the armlet on the left arm is present now. His lower lip has turned red due to continuous sighs. How his eyes have slackened due to keeping awake for the whole night.

In spite of melancholy, he does not appear weak, just as a chiseled huge gem gets small but looks splendid due to enhanced shining.

Sanumati : (seeing the king) Although the king has done great dishonour to Shakuntala by deserting her, it is understandable why Shakuntala restlessly yearns for the king. This king is very good looking.

King : (roams about and highly worried) When my beloved, deer-eyed Shakuntala was explaining to me again and again, I was somnolent and my eyes did not open. And see now, my quiescent heart has awakened only to bear the pain of remorse.

Sanumati : What to do now? Such is the bad luck of poor Shakuntala!

Jester : (separately) Oh! This disease called Shakuntala has seized our great king again. Don't know when he will get rid of this disease.

Chamberlain : (going close to great king) Victory to great king! Great king! The land of Pramad forest has been dusted and cleaned. Now, you can relax on the blissful land of this charming place for as long as you want.

King : Vetravati! Go and tell to *arya* Pishun the administrative officer, that I had woken up late today. Therefore, I would not be able to decide lawsuits in the assembly house today. Tell *arya* Pishun to write the tasks and issues of subjects that are to be looked into. Tell him to send that document to me.

Vetravati : As per the command of the great king!

[Vetravati departs]

King : Vatayan! Go, and carry on with your job.

Chamberlain : As per the command of *dev*.

[Chamberlain also goes away]

Jester : You have done a good deed by flying off all the flies from here. Now, entertain your mind by proceeding to the Pramad forest. It is neither chill nor winter of heat of summer there.

King : Yes friend! Someone has said rightly that adversity always looks for an opportunity. Those words were not wrong. Now See! I had hardly overcome the intoxication of forgetting Shakuntala when cupid has come again to excite me.

Jester : Well, you wait for some time. I shall break these Cupid's arrows with my rod (tries to shake off mango blooms).

King : (laughs) Well, let it go. I have witnessed your divine refulgence. Now move and find out a place where I could cool my eyes by seeing the vines resembling my beloved.

Jester : But, just a while ago, you had told Chaturika, the attendant of the harem, to fetch the incomplete drawing of Shakuntala made by you at Madhavi arbour.

King : Yes, I can recall that incidents. That is the place for entertainment. Alright, then, proceed towards that place.

Jester : Then, come this way, O great king! This way.

[Both turn and Sanumati follows them]

[Change of scene]

Jester : Look at it. This madhavi arbour is eagerly awaiting you after decorating this gem rock with flowers. Therefore proceed and sit on this flower-decked gem rock.

[Both enter and sit on the gem rock]

Sanumati : I shall keep a watch on them from the cover of vine. Let me see, what kind of image he has drawn of my confidante. After that, I will be able to tell my confidante how her husband is getting overwhelmed by her love.

[Goes behind the vine cover]

King : Friend! Now, all incidents and events related to Shakuntala are coming to memory. I had already told you about those things at the *ashram* of Kanva *rishi*. You were there when I had Shakuntala. But you had not brought those things to my memory. It seems that you had also forgotten all that, just like me.

Jester : Great king! I had not forgotten anything. But, while seeing me off, you said that you had given those statements jokingly, not seriously. Then, my stupid brain, had believed you. Or, it should be said that destiny is very powerful.

Sanumati : Yes, it is true.

King : (after thinking for a while of separation from her) Friend, now try to save me from this terrible agony.

Jester : What are you saying? It does not behove of people like you. Virtuous man should never be drowned in the ocean of sorrows. Mountains stand unmoved even on the arrival of tempest and storm; who can shake them?

King : Friend! I cannot control myself after recalling the condition of my beloved, I can't forget the moment when I had returned her disrespectfully from here.

When she was sent back from here and her companions, the disciples of the *guru*, as revered as *guru* himself, asked her sternly to stay back. At that moment she stopped there. At that moment, she had looked at me, a heartless fellow, with tearful eyes. That look is giving me pain as if someone has inflicted a wound on my body with a poison-drenched weapon!

Sanumati : (thinking) Oh! So much remorse for his deed! My mind is deriving great satisfaction at this time upon seeing the king's suffering.

Jester : Great king! It seems to me that some heavenly angel must have lifted *devi* Shakuntala at that time.

King : NO! Nobody can touch that faithful woman. I have heard at the *ashram* that Menka, the celestial damsel, had given birth to her. Therefore I guess that her compeers might have picked her up.

Sanumati : Aha! So, many of things are coming to the memory of the king. Anybody can be surprised by listening to them. But I am surprised to learn how he forget his past when Shakuntala was narrating the details to him.

Jester : Great king! If that is so, be assured that you two are going to be united soon.

King : Why? How can you say this?

Jester : Because no mother, father, or relative can tolerate that her or his daughter may remain separated from her husband. They will certainly do something.

King : Friend! My mind is getting confused. I am unable to understand correctly if the union with Shakuntala was a dream, magic or illusion. Or was it the reward of some holy deed whose fruit was enjoyed by me till the time up to which I was destined to enjoy it. After recollecting these things, I feel that all my hopes have scattered like a waterfall without any banks.

Jester : No, such thoughts of yours are correct. That is because the re-emergence of this ring proves that you are certainly going to meet with her.

King : (seeing the ring) Alas! I am feeling great pity for this ring too which had slipped from its right place. How could it slip away after reaching such a beautiful place?

[Seeing the ring]

O ring! It seems that the reward of your good deeds too had come to an end due to which you had fallen down. Otherwise, why should you fall off from the fingers having beautiful nails?

Sanumati : (thinking) The king is right. Had the ring fallen into the hands of someone else, his condition would have become very, very pathetic.

Jester : O great king! At least, tell me about how this ring, having your name, had reached *devi* Shakuntala.

Sanumati : *Wah*! The jester's mind is as curious to know about this topic as mine.

King : Listen carefully. When I was returning to my city from the *ashram*, my beloved had asked me with tears in her eyes, "After how many days would you enquire about me?"

Jester : Well, then! What was your answer?

King : At that time, I had put this ring into her finger and said, "Beloved! Keep counting the letters of my name, carved on this ring everyday. The day you would have counted all the letters, the same day, an attendant from my harem would be present here to invite you."

However, since I was stone-hearted, this invitation could not be sent to her.

Sanumati : It was a grand plan but the divine design spoiled it all.

Jester : How did it reach the stomach of the *rohu* fish that the fisherman had cut?

King : When Shakuntala was paying obeisance with folded hands at the pilgrim, this ring had slipped from her finger and flown with the stream of the Ganges.

Jester : Alright, now I have understood.

Sanumati : (thinking) That was the reason why this *rajarshi* had raised doubt about the matter of marriage with poor Shakuntala. He nurtured fear of committing *adharma* (sin). Otherwise, does any one need clarification in such kind of love. But how did this happen?

King : Now, I reproach this ring.

Jester : (thinking) Seems that our king is going crazy.

King : O ring! How could you jump off into the water, leaving the hand with beautiful and tender fingers? But the ring was lifeless, therefore, it was not wrong if it appreciated Shakuntala's hand and finger. But I am a human. How could I give disrespect to my beloved?

Jester : (thinking) My hunger will eat me up if the great king remains in this condition for some more time.

King : Dear! I am burning because of the repentance generated by deserting you; I did so without any reason. Therefore, soothe my wounds by kindly visiting me.

[An attendant enters raising the curtain with a picture board in hand]

Chaturika : Great king! Here is the image of *devi* drawn by you.

[Shows the picture board]

Jester : (thinking) Very good, my friend! Very beautiful. Upon seeing the contours drawn in this image, it seems to me that my eyes are stumbling. You have drawn her body so beautifully that her expressions are being accurately reflected through it.

Sanumati : *Rajarshi* is a very astute artiste. Upon seeing this image. I can visualize that my confidante Shakuntala herself is standing here.

King : Although I have corrected all the faults of this image to the best of my knowledge, yet the beauty of that *devi* has not descended completely in this sketch.

Sanumati : It behoves of this king lover to say all this due to remorse and humility. Otherwise, the picture has been made perfect.

Jester : Friend! Three *devi*s can be seen in this picture. And all the three are better than the other. Now, you tell me who is *devi* Shakuntala among them?

Sanumati : He is a fool; he has no eyes for beauty.

King : Well, you tell me first. Which one is Shakuntala among these?

Jester : I understand that the one who appears weary and is standing sticking to the mango tree, which is shining due to water sprinkles in this picture, should be Shakuntala. Flowers are falling from her hair. The drops of perspiration are visible on her face and further, both of her shoulders appear stooped. The other two ladies, who are visible here, should probably be her compeers.

King : Friend! You are truly an assayer. Have a look. The black spots of my sweating fingers have come up on the border of the picture and similarly, the colour on Shakuntala's cheek has been produced due to the tear that had fallen from my eyes. *Chaturikey!* The image of this recreation ground is incomplete. Go, and bring the brush, so I may be able to complete the picture.

Chaturika : *Arya* Madhavya! Kindly hold this picture board. I shall come back.

King : Leave it; I will hold it myself.

[Takes the picture board]

[Chaturika departs]

King : (heaving a deep sigh) Friend! Just look at my condition. I had packed her off after insulting her, when she had come to me. Now, I am expressing so much love towards her image. It is as if a deer were towards after shimmering sand considering it water but ignoring the water filled river.

Jester : (thinking) Here my great king is inclined towards mirage ignoring the river. (Overtly) Friend! What is left now to be drawn in this picture?

Sanumati : (thinking) I understand that the king will now draw those places in this picture which were very dear to my confidante.

King : Listen carefully. I have yet to draw the river, Malini, where a pair of swans were engaged in amorous play on the sand. I have to show the valley of the Himalaya as on both sides of the river, Malini, where deer should be doing regurgitation. Nearby, I want to draw one such tree where a *valkal* (garment made of bark) would be hanging. Under that tree, a deer couple would be sitting. The doe would be scratching her left eye with the horn of her black partner.

Jester : (within his heart) I understand that this picture should now be filled with hermits having long locks and beard.

King : Friend! There is more to it. I have forgotten to draw those ornaments, which I wanted to make my beloved wear.

Jester : What were those ornaments?

Sanumati : It could be only those ornaments that forest-dweller maidens like her used to wear.

King : At present, I have forgotten to draw that *Shireesh* flower which she had adorned on her ears at that time. The pollen of that flower had scattered on her cheeks. That is not all, I have yet not drawn the garland made of lotus fibers; it is as thin as the ray of the moon passing through the middle of her bosoms.

Jester : Why has this *devi* been shown scared, covering her face with her palm? (seeing the picture again with attention) And watch, this mean blackbee, greedy to us drink flower nectar, is hovering ceaselessly over the face of *devi*.

King : Drive off this shameless creature.

Jester : Great king! It is your job to punish the wretched ones; now only you should drive it off.

King : You are correct. O, dear guest to flowers and vines! Why are you taking pain to hover over her face? Look there, the female blackbee, eager for your love, is sitting on that flower gazing at you. Totally faithful to you, she is not drinking the flowers' juice without you.

Sanumati : (thinking) Even in this condition, how sweetly the great king is asking the blackbee to go away from there.

Jester : Great king! Do such vicious people listen to words?

King : (to blackbee) Why don't obey me? Then, listen to me.

My beloved's lips, are sanguine like tender blossoms of untouched tiny plants and which I had sipped very sparingly even during coitus. And if you dared to even touch these pomegranate like lips of hers, I shall put you inside a lotus and arrest you.

Jester : Hey black bee, are you not afraid of the one who can give you such a harsh punishment?

(laughing within his heart) O dear, he has gone mad already. But it seems to me that I have also become somewhat like him in his company.

(Overtly) Great king! It is only an image.

King : What? Is it an image?

Sanumati : (thinking) I have also understood only now that it was an image. He had made this picture absorbed in the thought of my dear confidante Shakuntala!

King : Friend! What an evil deed have you committed? I was enjoying with great attention the sight of real Shakuntala who was standing in front of me. But, by reminding me of the reality, you have reduced my beloved into mere image.

[King starts shedding tears]

Sanumati : This is quite a strange form of separation. Earlier, it was different and now, it is something else.

King : Friend! You can understand what has happened to my heart? Listen carefully. I am unable to meet her in my dream due to sleeplessness and these perennially flowing tears do not allow me to see her properly in the picture too.

Sanumati : You have washed up with your these words all the agony that you had infused in our heart by deserting Shakuntala.

[Entry of a female attendant]

Chaturika : Victory to the great king. With the box of painting material, I was coming this way when...

King : Well, what happened then?

Chaturika : Queen Vasumati appeared there the very moment accompanied by Taralika. After seizing the box from my hand, she said that she would deliver it to the great king herself.

Jester : It was only your good fortune that she did not thrash you.

Chaturika : Then, the queen's mantle got entangled with a branch of the tree and Taralika try to disentangle it. At that time I came here to give this news to you.

King : It seems that the queen is angry. She is coming this way in great fury. In this situation, it would be better not to show her this picture. Therefore, hide it at a place far away from queen's sight.

[The jester rises with the picture board]

Jester : Well, call me from the *Megh-Pratichhnad* house or come there yourself when you find freedom from the clutches of the queen.

[Departs from there hastily]

Sanumati : The king has given away his heart. But he does not want to hurt queen's heart. The truth is that not even an iota of love is left in his heart for this queen.

[Entry of doorkeeper with a letter in hand]

Doorkeeper : Victory to the King!

King : Vetravati! Did you see the queen while you were coming this way?

Doorkeeper : Yes sir, I did meet her. But she returned upon seeing this letter in my hand.

King : She has good judgment of time. She does not want that my work should suffer in any way due to her.

Doorkeeper : Great king! The minister has sent message that his full time was spent looking after arrangements of funds. Therefore, he was unable to do any other task. He has written in detail in this letter about the piece of work regarding the States subjects that have taken place, besides some other matters. After reading it you become aware of the situation.

King : Where is the letter? Bring it to me.

[Doorkeeper presents the letter]

King : (reading the letter) Oh, What is this? The boat of marine trader, Sarthhwah Dhanmitra, has sunk and he has died in the mishap. The poor man does not have even a progeny. And our minister is writing that his property should be attached to the royal treasury. How painful it is to be childless. Vetravati! *Setthji* was a very rich man. He might be having many wives. One of them might be pregnant. You tell me after examining this.

Vetravati : *Dev*! It has been heard that the daughter of the wealthy merchant of Saket, whom he had married, had observed the ritual of *punsavan* a few day's ago. So, it can be understood that she is in the family vase.

King : If that is the case, go and inform the minister that the child born from the womb of Dhanmitra's wife only would be the inheritor of the property of the *setth*. He should not hasten to attach the property with the royal treasury.

Vetravati : As be the King's command.

[Departs]

King : (asking to stop) Well, come here.

Vetravati : Sir, please give me the order.

King : What difference does it make whether someone has child or not?

Ask the minister to make a proclamation. Barring evil people, all people in our subjects should not be disappointed if they lose their kin. Dushyant is kin to all of them.

Doorkeeper : Great king! I shall arrange for this proclamation.

[Returns after some time]

Doorkeeper : Great king! After listening to your proclamation, the public has become happy. The king's rule is being praised everywhere.

King : (heaving a sigh) Some people die without progeny. Their wealth goes to others when they die. After my demise, the wealth of the Puru dynasty shall also meet the same fate.

Doorkeeper : May God never show such an ominous day.

King : (thinking) I am the one who has disregarded the *Lakshmi* who had visited my home on her own. I ought to be condemned, for I am the unfortunate one.

Sanumati : Now, there should be no doubt in it that this time the king has condemed himself, keeping Shakuntala in mind.

King : If timely sowed, the earth yields fruits. However, impregnated by me, my wife who would have run my family, has been disrespectfully deserted by me.

Sanumati : Nevertheless, your progeny shall carry on your dynasty.

Chaturika : (in isolation, with Vetravati) Vetravati! After listening the news of the demise of marine trader, Sarthhwah Dhanmitra, the sorrow of our king has doubled. Therefore, to save him from this condition, you go to *Megh-Pratichhnad* house and call Maadhavya. His mind would change in his presence and then, his grief would also lessen to some extent.

Doorkeeper : Yes, you are right.

[Departs]

King : Dushyant's forefathers would also be in great quandary. That is because they would be thinking who would offer the homage through Vedic tradition to them after the death of Dushyant. In this deliberation, with one part of the water from my offering they would be washing their tears and would slake their thirst from the remaining part of it.

[The king becomes unconscious]

Chaturika : (nervous) Great king! Have patience, have patience.

Sanumati : Alas! The king is suffering from the delusion of mind just as darkness spreads due to obstruction of small object on the path of a lamp, despite of it is illuminated. What should I do? I could have removed his worry right away but I am under obligation.

Assuring Shakuntala, Aditi had said that deities, eager to participate in the *yajna* (sacrificial fire), would arrange union of Dushyant and her.

I think that it is not proper to delay anymore. I must tell all these things to Shakuntala at once so that the she might become assured.

[Thus Sanumati flies off]

[In the background]

Oh! He has hurt me. He has hurt a brahmin.

King : (listens attentively) Hey, this is Madhavya's voice.

Is there anyone?

[Doorkeeper enters]

Doorkeeper : (in worrisome voice) Great king! Your friend has fallen in great trouble. Kindly move and save him.

King : Who is troubling Madhavya?

Doorkeeper : Great king! It is beyond comprehension. It seems as if some evil spirits have caught him. After lifting him up, it has hanged him over the parapet of *Megh-Pratichhnad* house.

[King rises]

King : How is that possible? Have the evil spirits started making my palace their place of stay? Yes! It may be possible.

That is because when man does not know himself, how many sinful acts he has done, how can then it be known who among my subjects is doing what and when? Who has the power to know this?

[In the background]

Hey friend! Save me, save me.

[King leaves hastily]

King : Friend! Do not fear, do not fear.

[In the background]

Hai! Oh my! Ah! How should I not be afraid? I don't know who is here twisting my neck just like one would do to a sugarcane fruit.

[King looks around]

King : Where is my bow?

[The doorkeeper enters with bow and arrow]

Yawani : *Swami!* Take it, here is your bow and arrow.

[King takes bow and arrow]

[In the background]

Thirsty of your warm blood oozing from your throat, I will execute you in the same way as a lion kills animals after giving them extreme pain. I shall see how king Dushyant, the protector of tormented ones, comes to save you.

King : (angrily) So, are you challenging even me? You eater of carrion, devil! You just wait. Your time is up. I shall decimate you right away.

[King pulls the bowstring]

Vetravati! Show me the path with stairs. You move ahead, I am following you.

Doorkeeper : Great king! Come, come this way.

[All depart hastily]

King : (seeing around) There is nothing here, no one is visible anywhere.

[In the background]

Hai! Help me, help me! I can see you but you are not seeing me. Like a mouse, stuck in the clutches of a cat, loses hope of life, I have lost hope of living.

King : O, you are proud of the art of impostering! Now only my arrow will see you. Here I load the arrow. As a swan separates water from the milk mixed with water, this arrow of mine will kill you. That is because you are worthy of being killed. I will save this Brahmin, who is worthy of being protected.

[Saying this, the king loads the arrow]

[At that moment enters, Matali enters leaving the jester]

Matali : (says to the king) Indra has entrusted this bow and arrow to execute demons just like deer. Now, you should aim these arrows at those demons. That is so because such gentlemen as you, do not rain arrows on their friends; rather, they shower kindness on them.

King : (putting off the arrow from the bow, looks in surprise) O Matali! The charioteer of Indra, come! you are welcome.

[The jester enters]

Jester : He was going to kill me as a sacrificial animal; that is why, he is being felicitated here. This is great atrocity!

Matali : (smiling) *Ayushman!* First, listen to me and learn my Indra *maharaj* has sent me to you.

King : Yes, speak. I am listening attentively.

Matali : Great king! A demon named Kalnemi was born in the ancient period.

King : Yes, I have heard his name and all his deeds. Wasn't that a matter of the past?

Matali : That was what I was telling you. Although Kalnemi was present in an ancient period, his descendants do belong to this period. His descendants have formed a squad that is not being controlled by anyone. They have become indomitable.

King : Yes, Naradji had told me about this long ago. But he did not tell who was suffering due to them. That is why I could not take any action.

Matali : Now listen great king! Even your friend, Indra, has become incapable at present. He had tried to conquer them but could not do so. So, it has been rightly understood that only you can defeat them in the battlefield. The reason is that the sun, riding his seven-horse chariot, cannot defeat the darkness of the night that only moon can defeat. Therefore, having this bow and arrow, riding Indra's chariot you depart for victory now.

King : I am grateful for this kindness of lord Maghawa. So, I proceed now. But tell me why did you behave with poor Madhavya in this fashion?

Matali : When I arrived here, I found that you appeared slightly indisposed but I could not find out the cause. Then, I deemed fit that your anger should be ignited to drive away your indisposition. So I did what I understood proper at that time. It turns into flame only when the fuel is shaken vigorously. Similarly, the snake raises his hood and hisses only when someone agitates him. In the same way, a man remembers his strength and brilliance when some one provokes or challenges him.

King : (to the Jester) Friend! Lord Indra's command is final. Who can alter that?

Jester : (worried) Yes, then?

King : Then means that you must go to minister Pishun.

Jester : Then?

King : Then tell him that my bow is engaged in some other task at present. As long as it is busy, he should protect the subjects according to his wisdom. That is all.

Jester : As you command.

[Departs]

Matali : Proceed *Ayushman*! Climb on the chariot.

[King acts as if ascending the chariot]

[All depart]

•

Act VII

[Entry of king and Matali, through the air route, both sitting on the chariot]

King : Matali! I had obeyed only the command of Indra *maharaj*. But he has accorded grand hospitality to me even though my service was a trifle in comparison. I am feeling quite like helpless.

Matali : (smiling) *Ayushman*! I have come to discuss something else.

King : What is that?

Matali : That both of you have not got tired at all by seeing each other. In spite of accomplishing such a major task for Indra, you are saying that it was a trifle. The sole reason for this is that you want to pay grand honour to Lord Indra. And Indra, on the other side, is so astounded by your valor that he considers, despite extending sufficient hospitality to you, that he has not been able to extend proper welcome that could be up to your status.

King : Matali! No, it is not so. The honour accorded to me during send-off was so grand that I could never have imagined such an honour. He made me sit with him on one half of his throne in the presence of all gods. Then, he took off the garland of *mandaar* (consisting of divine sandalwood and adorning his chest). He put that garland around my neck with great pleasure. Even Jayant was looking greedily at this *mandaar* garland.

Matali : *Ayushman*! At least tell me which honour is there that you do not deserve to receive from Indra, the king of gods? There have only been two persons who have always spent comfortable life like Indra and uprooted the demons from the heaven.

King : (interrupting) Who were those two great warriors?

Matali : In the ancient period, it was Lord *Narasimha* who had torn off the stomach of Hiranyakashipu, the enemy of gods, with his nails.

King : (interrupting again) And the second one?

Matali : You are the second one who has eliminated demons from the Indralok with his sharp arrows.

King : Matali! All this is the result of the greatness of lord Indra; I was merely a medium. Now, listen carefully. If one's servant accomplished a great task, it should be understood that one's swami has honoured him by giving responsibility of such a task and that alone should be considered to be one's reward. If the Sun does not carry scarlet glow preceding it, where is the capability in the scarlet glow alone to dispel the darkness?

Matali : This is your magnanimity. It behoves of you to talk like that.

[Moving a little forward]

Ayushman! See the overwhelming influence of your glory which has unfurled in the heaven. Singing your eulogy in songs, gods are illustrating your heroic tale on the clothes made of the vines of *kalp* tree.

King : Matali! My sole attention was to fight with demons when I had come here. Therefore, I could not see the route to heaven properly as I was absorbed in achieving my objective. Now, kindly tell me which layer of the air are we cruising through?

Matali : I can explain, O king. We, at present, are cruising though the layer which God had sanctified by putting his second step during his *vaman* incarnation. Here blows the air named *pariwah* in which moves the Milky Way. This is the very layer which guides stars properly with its air streams.

King : Matali! Now I have understood.

Matali : What?

King : That, upon reaching here, that all my senses, along with the soul, have become joyful. That is so because we are sailing through the layer where air named *pariwah* and Milky Way flow.

[Watches the wheels of the chariot and says]

It appears that we have arrived at the part of the sky where clouds float.

Matali : How did you come to know this?

King : Look! The wheel of your chariot has become wet due to water; it can be understood from this that we are sailing on clouds saturated with water. The horses of our chariot also appear gleaming due to flash of lightning. Moreover, Chataks, the birds that subsist only on precious rain drop, are flying through the spokes of our chariot wheels.

Matali : *Ayushman*! Now you would land on the ground of your kingdom in a few moments.

King : (looking downwards) Matali! How strange does this human world lying below appear? Isn't it so?

Matali : How?

King : At present, it seems as if the land were descending from the high peaks of mountains! The branches of tree, which were hidden so far by leaves, have also become visible now.

Now look! There are thin lines from a distance. They are widening now and shaping into rivers. Further, this earth seems as if it were rising towards us or as if someone were throwing it upwards.

Matali : Your comparison is correct. Actually this is the truth. It is a very strange spectacle. (seeing with reverence) Wow! How charming this earth appears to be.

King : Matali! Tell me which mountain is this that is spread through eastern to western coast, appearing long and wide and spreading golden trail like a wall of evening clouds?

Matali : *Ayushman!* This is the inhabitance of *kinnar*s, whereby observing ascetic practices, people acquire fulfillment soon. This is the mountain named Hemkut. Prajapati Kashyap the father of gods and demons, son of self-styled Mareechi, sitting with his wife. He is in deep meditation.

King : This is a matter of great luck for me. An auspicious occasion that comes to hand should not be missed.

Matali : What?

King : I will offer *pradakshinaa* (reverential salutation by moving around a deity from left to right) to lord Kashyap; we will proceed after that only.

Matali : You have taken an appropriate devision, O king!

[Both act as if getting down from chariot]

King : (astonished) I could not make out when your chariot came down. That is because while touching the ground, I neither heard of the clatter of wheels nor dust. Further, you did not pull the reins either. When did it stop?

Matali : That is the only difference between the chariot of *Ayushman* and that of Indra.

King : Matali! Where is the *ashram* of the great *muni* Kashyap, the son of Mareechi?

Matali : (indicating with hand) That it is, the *ashram* of Kashyap *rishi*. He has been undertaking such a tough meditation *(tapasya)* there that ant hills have formed up to cover one half of his body. Innumerable snake sloughs are sticking to his chest. Dry creeping plants are hanging around his neck. Birds have formed nests in his tresses. And he, the *Prajapati,* is such, a great sage that he has been observing the meditation ritual by staring at sun.

King : I offer salutation to the great soul observing such a great austerity.

[Matali acts to stop the chariot by pulling the reins]

Matali : Great king! We have arrived at *prajapati* Kashyap's *ashram.* Look, this beautiful array of *mandaar* trees has been planted by Aditi with her own hands.

King : Peace is even more profound here than the heaven. I have begun to feel as if I have jumped into a pool of nectar!

[Matali acts to stop the chariot]

Matali : *Ayushman!* Get down.

[Kings acts to descend]

King : Matali! What would you do now?

Matali : I have stopped the chariot. Now I am also getting down along with you.

[Descends]

Matali : Come this way, *Ayushman*! This way. (Wandering) Come, see the sacred grove of *rishi*s here.

King : Actually, I am greatly surprised upon seeing all this. These ascetics are observing meditation rituals *(tapasya)* amidst those things the other *rishi*s aspire to achieve. Here they live by breathing the invigorating air of the forest of *kalp* trees. They pray and worship after taking dip in water soaked with lotus pollen. They meditate sitting on the gem rocks and observe celibacy with rigorous *tapasya* amidst celestial damsels.

Matali : The objectives of such great men happen to be comparably lofty.

[Turning towards sky]

Tell, elderly Shakalya*ji*! What is the great soul, *rishi* Kashyap, doing at present?

What did you say? Dakshayami had asked him a question regarding the *dharma* of faithfulness to one's husband *(pativrat)*. The answer she had obtained from Kashyap was sought to be known by other *rishi* wives. The *rishi* is sitting close to those *rishi* wives and repeating that answer for them.

King : (listens attentively) Oh! this is such a narrative that I must have to stay here to listen to it, until it concludes.

Matali : (looking towards the king) Until I seek an opportunity to inform *maharshi* Kashyap, the father of Indra, to inform about your arrival, you proceed and sit under the Ashoka tree.

King : As you suggest.

[Acts to sit down]

Matali : *Ayushman*! I am going.

[He goes away.]

King : (seeing an auspicious time) I have no hope of the fulfillment of my wish. Still, O my arm! Why are you fluttering unnecessarily? It is truth that one, who rejects *Lakshmi* at his door, repents later.

[In the background]

Brother! Leave these pranks. Why are you again bent upon showing your old traits?

[King listens attentively]

King : This is an *ashram* where immodesty has no place. Who is hell-bent upon doing mischief?

[The king looks in that direction with surprise]

Hey, Who is this courageous boy? Two female hermits are coming behind him.

The cubs have not adequately fed themselves with milk from their mother's teats. That boy is pulling the cubs apart and forcing them to play with him. In this tussle, his locks have been disheveled.

[A child enters with female hermits]

Child : (lisping) O lion! Open your mouth; I will count your teeth.

First Female Hermit : *O* prankster! Why do you harass those who we have reared as our children? *Ha*! Your pranks are growing day by day.

The *rishi*s have named you Sarvadaman. Plausibly, they would have given you this name after thorough deliberation.

[King sees the child]

King : I don't know why affection is swelling in my heart exactly in the same way as it happens upon seeing one's own legitimate son. Possibly, since I do not have any child of my own, therefore such feelings might be swelling in my heart.

Second Female Hermit : Look, if you did not spare these cubs, the lioness, their mother, will attack you.

Child : (smiling and, in prattling tone) Oops! she is very frightening; I am scared upon seeing her.

[The child makes a wry face and twists his lips to mock at the female hermits]

King : This child appears to be the son of a brilliant, great man. He looks like the spark which is awaiting fuel to create divine flames.

First Female Hermit : Son! Spare this lion's cub. I shall fetch some other toy for you to play.

[The child puts forth his hand]

Child : Where is the toy, bring it to me.

King : (Looking at the child's hand) *Oh*! The signs of sovereign kings can be seen on his hand. Spread for a toy, this palm looks like the lone lotus which shines with the reddishness of daybreak and which has yet not bloomed fully.

Second Female Hermit : Suvrata! Do you think that you can make him swallow the bait? It is impossible. Go and bring the peacock painted by the *rishi*-son, Markandeya, kept at my cottage.

First : Alright.

[Departs]

Child : (lisping) Alright, I will play with it until then.

[Bursts into laughter upon seeing the female hermit]

King : I don't know why, this naughty child seems to be so dear to me. Blessed shall be that person in whose lap this jovial child would be sitting. Blessed that woman to who, this could, with bud-like teeth and lisping voice, would be putting the diet of his body on her body.

Female Hermit: But he does not pay heed to my instruction.

[Looks around]

Is any *rishi* son present here?

(upon seeing the king)

Gentleman! Will you slightly come forward and help release this lion's cub from the hands of this child? He does not count me at all. He has held it so strongly that I am unable to release it from this child's hands. It will stifle to death that way.

[King goes near]

King : (smiling) O revered *maharshi's* son!

Why are you doing such deeds against the rules of the *ashram?* These poor creatures have been living comfortably and simply at this *ashram* since birth. You are harassing them.

Female Hermit: Gentleman! This child is not the son of a *rishi*.

King : True, the way he acts also, his look and shape appearance give indication that he is not the son of a *rishi*. But I have called him the son of a *rishi* as I have seen him here, at the *ashram*.

[The king affectionately pats the child]

King : (thinking) I don't know which family this child belong to. If his mere touch can offer me such delight, how delightful it would be to take him in my lap.

[Female hermit watches the two]

Female Hermit: Surprise, great surprise!

King : *Arye*! What is the surprising element in it?

Female Hermit : He is similar to you. This child gives me surprise. Oh! He did not disobey you, although you were totally stranger. He has obeyed you what you have said.

[King showers affection for the child]

King : If he is not *rishi*'s son, who is he then? Please tell me about him.

Female Hermit : He is offspring of Puru dynasty.

[The king is shocked]

King : (thinking) Is he from my family? That is why this female hermit is telling that his features resemble mine. But that is the tradition of Puru dynasty protecting the earth, they inhabit royal palaces, full of affluence, during their youth and go during old age, along with their faithful wife, to live in forest.

[Overtly]

But people inhabiting the earth cannot reach here at their will. Then, how did this child come here?

Female Hermit : You are right. His mother is the daughter of a celestial damsel, therefore, she has given birth to him at the *ashram* of god's *guru*, Mareechi.

King : (thinking) *Arey*, There is another ray of hope for me. Well, tell me which *rajarshi*'s wife is that *devi*?

Female Hermit: (making wry face) *Tch!, Tch*! Who would like to utter the name of that wily king who has deserted his wife?

King : (thinking) These words of the female hermit seem to be applicable to me. If that is so, I better ask the name of the child's parents with her. But would it be decent to ask about a strange woman in this fashion.

[Female hermit returns with a clay toy]

Female Hermit : (to the child) Sarvadaman! See the beauty of the child Shakuntala.

[The child looks around]

Child : Where is my mother?

Female Hermits : He is so attached to his mother that he is baffled by merely listening the sound of his mother's name.

Other Female Hermit : Child! please see the beauty of this clay peacock.

King : (thinking) Does this mean that his mother's name is Shakuntala? But there could be several namesakes in this big world. This name has come up to add to my sorrows?

Child : (in his lisping tone) *Arya*! This peacock is very nice.

[Takes the toy]

First Hermit : (looks worrisome) The armlet, which was tied on his arm like a protector shield, is not seen visible.

King : Do not worry. It had fallen when he was playing with the lion's cub.

[Tries to pick up]

Both : (worried) No, do not touch it. (with surprise) *Hey*! He has picked it up.

[Look at each other]

King : (astonished) Why did you try to stop me from picking it up?

First Female Hermit: Listen *maharaj*! *Maharshi* Mareechi had given him this medicine, named *Aparajita*. Tying it around his arm, he had said that nobody but his parents should lift it if it falls down on the earth somehow.

King : What would happen if someone else lifted it?

First Female Hermit: Then, this armlet would then turn into a serpent and it would immediately bite the person who picks it up from the ground.

King : Did you ever see such a thing happening?

Female hermit: Yes, why not? I have seen it a number of times.

King : (delightfully thinking) Why should I not be too glad!

[Hugs the child close to his chest]

Second Female Hermit : *Suvratey!* Come and reveal this good news to Shakuntala.

[Both depart]

Child : (in a lisping voice) Leave me, I will go to my mother.

King : Son! Now you give joy to your mother accompanying me.

Child : (in a lisping tone) You are not my father. My father is king Dushyant.

King : (smiling) This argument is strengthening my belief.

[Shakuntala enters]

Shakuntala : I could not believe my luck after listening that the shrub fallen from Sarvadaman's arm did not turn into a snake upon being picked up from the ground. Or, it could be possible that what Sanumati had said was right.

[King sees Shakuntala]

King : Here is! *Devi* Shakuntala. A pair of soiled clothes are on her body, her face has lost vigor observing austerity, her hair is in one lock, and she has been doing meditaton *(tapasya)* with pure heart for so long in the separation of a pitiless like me.

Shakuntala : (upon seeing the remorseful king) He does not look like *Aryaputra*. Who is he then? Embracing my son, under the protection of that sacred thread, he is soiling his own body.

[Upon seeing his mother, the child goes to her]

Child : (lisping) Mother! See, here is a man who calls me his son and is embracing me.

King : Beloved! It is the punishment of the cruelty which I had committed against you that you have not recognized me so far.

Shakuntala : (thinking) Hey, my heart! Have some patience. God has become kind to me, by mistake. Yes, he is *Aryaputra!*

King : Beloved! It is my great fortune that the cover of delusion has lifted from my memory today. You have appeared before me out of the blue. *Sumukhi!* You have met me in the same way as Rohini comes to meet the moon after the end of an eclipse.

Shakuntala : Victory to *Aryaputra*, victory to *Aryaputra*...

[The throat chokes meanwhile and she is not able to speak further]

King : Beauty! I have become the conqueror from the word 'victory' which you have uttered from your choked throat. That is because my eyes have seen your face today. Oh! Your beautiful lips have become pale.

Child : Mother! Who is he?

Shakuntala : Son! Ask your fortune.

[King falls on Shakuntala's feet]

King : Beauty! Remove the agony from your mind that I had dishonoured you. I also don't know where from the shadow of ignorance had engulfed me at that time. It is true that those, who happen to be *tamoguni,* make such mistakes in executing good tasks too.

Shakuntala : Rise *Aryaputra*! During those days, it certainly would have been effect of some of my sin from past birth. That is why such a kind *Aryaputra* had become averse to me.

[King rises]

Shakuntala : *Aryaputra*! But tell me how did you remember this petty, agonized woman?

King : Let me remove my thorn-like agony first. I shall tell you everything. O beauty! On that day your tear drops were flowing down your cheeks and hurting your lips. I had inadvertently insulted those precious tears on that day. The same tear drops are visible in your eyes even today.

Until I wipe them with my own hands my mind will not find peace.

[Wipes Shakuntala's tears with his hand]

Shakuntala : (upon seeing the ring in Dushyant's finger having his name) *Aryaputra*, this is your ring.

King : Yes, I was able to recollect all those incidents after getting this ring.

Shakuntala : It had really done a vicious act. When I was going to show it as proof to you, it had disappeared at the very moment. I don't know where it had fallen.

[King removes the ring and offers it to Shakuntala]

King : As the flowering of a vine indicates that the vine has met with the spring, you should also wear this ring as a symbol of our meeting.

Shakuntala : (holding him) No, no. Now, I have no faith in it. Let *Aryaputra* wear it.

[Matali enters]

Matali : Accept my greetings *Ayushman,* for meeting your legitimate wife and son.

King : Matali! My wish has been rewarded very sweetly. But Lord Indra might not be aware of all this.

Matali : (smiling) Well, can anything be beyond the knowledge of gods? *Ayushman,* come! Lord Mareechi wants to show himself to you.

King : Shakuntala! You hold the child. I want to see the sight of Lord Mareechi.

Shakuntala : I feel shy while going before elders with *Arya.*

King : One must move together at the time of joy. Come now!

[All move towards one direction where Lord Mareechi is seated]

[Change of scene]

[Mareechi is seen seated with Aditi]

Mareechi : (upon seeing the king) Dakshayani! He is Dushyant.

He is the very king, Dushyant, who nurtures and feeds the entire world, and who remains in the front in every battle for your son, Indra. His arrows have accomplished so much that Indra's sharp-edged *Vajra* is adorning like his ornament.

Aditi : His valor can be judged from his stout physique.

Matali : *Ayushman*! These are parents of gods. They are watching you with such affection with which parents see their children. Move, go close to them.

King : Matali! Are they the ones who were born to Daksh and Mareechi one generation after Brahma. The *rishi*s accept them as the parents of all the twelve Adityas. Indra, who takes part in *yajna*, was born to them. Lord Brahma who takes birth on his own to do well to this world, also takes birth from them.

Matali : Exactly! what else did you think?

[The king goes closer]

King : Dushyant, who regularly obeys the command of Indra, offers salutation to you both.

Mareechi : Child! May you have a long life. Rear the earth, well and earn glory.

Aditi : Child! May you become matchless! May you become so strong that no enemy may be able to stand before you.

Shakuntala : I, along with my son, pay respect to you.

Mareechi : Child! Your husband is like Indra and your son is like Jayant. Therefore, I am puzzled; as what kind of blessing should I confer on you? Well, I bless you that you become as luminous as *Paulomee*, that is Indrani.

Aditi : Daughter! May you become the one who received respect from her husband. Your son may live long. He may give joy to both the families!

Come, sit down.

[All sit around *Prajapati*]

Mareechi : (Points towards all one by one) Today by fortune, this faithful Shakuntala, this great child and you all the three persons have met in such a way as if faith, wealth and action were meeting!

King : Lord! Your kindness is actually wonderful, where wish is accomplished first and the fortune to have your sight comes next. This is the actual sequence of cause and effect, first it flowers and then comes the fruit. In the same way, clouds come first and rain afterwards.

Matali : Those who are creators of fortune, precede his blessings.

King : Lord! I had married this obedient daughter of yours at one time by following *Gandharva* custom. When his kith and kin came to me with her a few days later, I don't know what had happened to my memory. I was not able to recognize her at that time. I had forgotten all the incidents. I had turned her back at that time, thus inflicting great dishonour on her.

I had committed a grave crime towards *maharshi* Kanva, of your clan, by doing so. However, when I found this ring, I noticed that my memory had returned that I had married the daughter of *maharshi* Kanva at his *ashram* under the *Gandharva* custom. All these things appear quite strange to me.

Mareechi : Child! Get rid of guilt from your mind completely because you cannot commit a mistake of this type. I shall tell to you what has happened.

King : Sir, I am listening.

Mareechi : When wailing Menaka along with Shakuntala had come to Dakshaayani while descending from *Apsara* pilgrim, I had learnt through meditation (*tapa*) that it was Durwasa's curse. Due to it, you had deserted your legitimate ascetic by not recognizing her. But Durwasa's curse was valid until you saw this ring. When you saw the ring, the curse became null and void.

[King takes breath of relief]

King : Finally, I was exculpated from the blame.

Shakuntala : (to herself) It is a matter of great fortune that *Aryaputra* had not deserted me for no reason. But I have no recollection of the events. So, I don't know when I committed such an error against *maharshi* Durwasa and when he invoked such a curse on me. Or, it is possible that I bore the curse but did not remember due to my separation from *rajarshi.* While departing from the *ashram,* my confidantes had told me that I should show this ring if the need arose.

Mareechi : Child! You have got the correct interpretation. Therefore, do not bear any anger or wrath against your husband. One cannot see one's image in a mirror that is covered with dust, but the image appears clear when the dust is removed. In the same way, the king had deserted you due to his lost memory owing to the curse. But now, when the curse has been removed, he has recognized as well as accepted you.

King : Lord is correct.

Mareechi : Child! We have thoroughly carried out all the rituals of Shakuntala's son so far. You tell us, have you accepted him or not?

King : Lord! This child who is going to run our dynasty.

[Lifts the child in his lap]

Mareechi : Child! He will indeed run your family. But he will also become sovereign emperor. Riding his strong and straight moving chariot, this child should conquer the earth, consisting of seven islands, all by himself in such a way that no warrior shall be able to stand before him.

He used to harass all the animals of this *ashram* very much. Therefore, he had acquired the name of Sarvadaman. But in the future, he will rear the world. Therefore, his name would be Bharat.

King : Lord! We shall expect that this child shall carry forward the culture and values inculcated by you in him.

Aditi : Lord! We must send the detailed description of the fulfillment of the wish of this girl to *maharshi* Kanva. Her mother Menaka, who loves her, has lived here and has served us very well.

Shakuntala : (thinking) The goddess has spoken my thought.

Mareechi : Dear lady! *Maharshi* Kanva knows all these things due to the effect of his *tapa* (austerity).

King : That is the reason why he did not get angry with me when I had offended dear Shakuntala.

Mareechi : Even then, we must send this message to him on our own. Hey, is there anybody here?

[Disciple enters]

Disciple : Lord! I am at your command.

Mareechi : Galav! Immediately you proceed to *maharshi* Kanva's *ashram* through the sky route and tell him on my behalf that Dushyant has recalled everything of his past after being free from curse. Further, tell him that he has accepted Shakuntala and her son.

Disciple : As per the command of the Lord.

[Departs]

Mareechi : Child! Riding the chariot of your friend, Indra, you too return to your capital along with your son and wife.

King : As per the command of the Lord.

Mareechi : Listen carefully.

May Indra always rain sufficiently for your subjects.

Ruling over hundreds of republics and carrying out numerous *yajnas*, you too keep Indra pleased. Thus, you both keep doing good deeds for each other so that both of you may live happily ever after!

King : Lord! I will always try to do good deeds due to your blessings.

Mareechi : Child! I have conferred blessings on you. Now, you may tell me if you have some wish that you would like to be fulfilled. Tell me, how I can be of use to you.

King : What else can be a greater wish than the blessing that you have conferred on my family and me. Even then, if you want to bestow more kindness upon me, then give me a boon that the kings should always remain engaged in the welfare of the masses, great scholars and poets and finally, the lord of all lords, who has created himself and spread his energies in all directions, should give such a blessing to us all that I may not have to come down to this mortal earth for rebirth.

[All leave]

• • •

www.ingramcontent.com/pod-product-compliance
Lightning Source LLC
LaVergne TN
LVHW010108170826
845678LV00012B/2295

* 9 7 8 8 1 2 8 8 2 4 5 3 1 *